DOWN HOME

STEVE L CLARK

Down Home
By Steve L Clark

Edited by Brandon Applegate

Cover art by Matt Wildasin

Interior Formatting by Brandon Applegate

ISBN 9781965316047

OTHER WORKS BY STEVE L CLARK

<u>Novellas</u>

The Doors of Chamberlain

<u>Short Story Collections</u>

The Collapse of Ordinary

<u>Anthologies</u>

Dark Words: Stories of Urban Legends and Folklore

Edited by Matt Wildasin

CONTENTS

For Mom

You asked for a ghost story, and there's some of that here, but it wouldn't be me if I didn't take it a little further. Some of the seeds in this story do grow on the mountain. Whether I pulled it from your stories or my own experiences, I hope you find pieces of down home.

CHAPTER 1

The cars winding through the narrow cemetery paths slowed as the hearse pulled over and parked. A blue canopy stood over the open grave. Passengers emerged from their vehicles, shambling in clusters toward the gravesite where the pastor stood waiting.

Paula Tompkins pulled in behind a pickup truck and shut off the ignition. She exhaled in relief. The six-hour trip from Ohio was filled with squeals and knocks of protest from her old Buick. The trip back home would be another challenge, but for the moment, she could relax. She stared out the window at the rolling green hills.

I can't believe I'm back here. Ten years ago she swore she'd never set foot on this mountain. There was only one thing that could bring her back—one good memory out of a lifetime of bad.

Aunt Candace. Paula left the holler the day she turned eighteen, and Candace was the only person she stopped to see on the way out. The visit was brief. Candace met her on the front porch with a sad smile. Before Paula could speak, Candace wrapped her up in a warm hug and pecked her on the cheek.

"I knew this day was coming, and you're right for leaving, but I'm gonna miss you, girl."

Paula hugged her fiercely in return and whispered promises to stay in touch. Then she headed north, her heart aching, yet bursting with hope for the future—away from the mountain, away from—

Home.

Home wasn't the right word. A home wasn't supposed to be filled with this much grief and anger. The mountain was the place she existed. She'd make a home somewhere else.

Home became Ohio. Crossing the river into Cincinnati, she'd felt like Dorothy lost in Oz. Her yellow brick road took her to Cousin Darrell's house. He was a few years older and blazed the path she followed out of the mountain. When she'd called and asked if she could stay until she got on her feet, he welcomed her with a standing invitation to stay as long as she liked. He had his own reasons for leaving, and didn't question hers.

She landed a job at a factory. After a few months spent saving, she signed a lease on a small apartment. Just like that, the quiet little girl from the mountain was making a life of her own.

Paula made good on her word and kept in touch with Candace. In the beginning, they sent letters back and forth. Several times they would meet halfway and get together in Lexington for lunch. It wasn't as frequent as either of them would like, but they did the best they could to stay connected.

When the call came, Paula'd had a bad feeling all morning. She'd picked up the ringing phone with irrational hesitation. Paula's uncle Larry greeted her with his gruff voice then delivered the news.

"Sorry to have to tell ya this, but Candy passed away this morning. Doc says it looks like a heart attack."

The color drained from her face as she was overcome with dizziness and nausea.

"I know you two were close. The funeral will be on Saturday. I hope you can make it. She would've wanted you to be there, I believe."

The thought of going back overwhelmed her, but despite herself, she said she would come. Larry wished her safe travel and hung up the phone. Paula stood in the kitchen, holding the phone to her chest, while tears streaked her cheeks.

That was three days ago.

Now, she was back, a stranger in a familiar land. The service was held at a small church not far from her childhood home. She'd gone there occasionally as a child, but church attendance from her family had been sporadic at best, especially after her mother passed. Paula grimaced as those memories threatened to emerge, and she shut it down, focusing on the beauty of the mountain. Nothing good would come from thinking back on those days.

A tap on the window startled her out of her memories. Uncle Larry's big face smiled down at her. Rosy cheeks popped out of a scraggly gray beard. The wrinkles had deepened since the last time she saw him, but his kind eyes still shined through. She smiled back and opened the car door. Larry looked uncomfortable in his black suit. The tie was crooked, and he tugged absently at the jacket.

"Good heavens, Paula, you're all grown up."

"You haven't changed a bit," Paula said.

"You're full of it, but I thank ya all the same," Larry said. He put his arm around her and hugged her gently to his side. "Real glad you could come down. I know Candy would've wanted you here. You meant a lot to her."

Paula nodded. Tears stung, threatening to spill over.

Larry gave her a sympathetic smile.

They walked together across the cemetery towards the blue tent. Paula studied the tombstones. This was the oldest section with stones dating back to the early 1800s. Even so, many of the surnames were ones she knew. Hollis. Carbury. Johnson. Fields. Sizemore. Cornett. These were all families she knew. Roots ran deep in the mountains. Once they took hold, it was hard to break free.

"Angie will be glad to see you," Larry said.

"She here? I must've missed her at the service."

"She had to work, but she'll be here for the burial. You should make time to talk to her. She was always enamored with you. She used to say she was gonna run off and chase her dreams like Paula." Larry chuckled. "Never did though. Seems happy enough. But I think part of her still wishes she followed you."

Paula nodded. Angie was a few years younger, and they hadn't been close as kids, but she was flattered to think she was anyone's role model.

"I'll do that. You may have to point her out to me though. She was just a little thing last time I saw her."

"Can't miss her. She looks like me without the beard."

Paula laughed and patted Larry's arm. In her pursuit to block out all the bad things that happened to her, she realized she might've given up some happy memories, too.

"Thank you for calling me, Uncle Larry." She looked around at the sprawling hills. "I think maybe I needed to come back. I wish it wasn't for Aunt Candy's funeral, but—"

"Yup," Larry said, "sometimes you need to see things with fresh eyes. Things aren't always the way you thought they were. Sometimes they are, sure, but sometimes what you remember isn't—*exactly* how it happened. You follow me?"

Paula furrowed her brow. She remembered *exactly* how things happened.

Larry noticed the shift in her features and winced.

"Now don't go thinking I'm sticking up for your daddy. He didn't live the best life, and I believe he knew and regretted it. Guess what I'm trying to say is family is important. These mountains are rooted in it, and nowhere I ever been felt like home except here." Larry scratched his head and cleared his throat. "There I go again, maybe not saying the right thing. I'm not judging you for leaving. You did what you needed to, and no one blames you for that. I'm hoping you'll see these old hills aren't quite as bad as you remember, and maybe you'll come see your old uncle Larry every now and then."

Paula smiled and wrapped him in a hug. "Thank you."

"You're welcome, sweet pea. Well, I think old Grover is about to get going, so let's get this business done and lay Candy to rest."

They joined the rest of the mourners around the grave. Larry shuffled his way to the front, while Paula kept her place in the back. She appreciated Larry's sentiment that no one blamed her for leaving, but she suspected that wasn't true. Several times throughout the service she noticed people giving her side glances and little frowns they thought went unnoticed. It didn't bother her much, but she found herself hoping there might be a few more people like Larry who were happy to see her. Friendly faces would make the trip more bearable.

The pastor fidgeted by the grave, compulsively checking his watch every few seconds. Paula didn't recognize him, but she knew his name was Grover, and he was her cousin. Second cousins once removed or something like that. He was short and balding, tiny framed glasses floating on his nose. He shifted his weight back and forth, from one foot to the other, like he couldn't bear to stand still.

The murmur of conversations trailed and died off. Grover nodded and cleared his throat.

"Let us pray."

CHAPTER 2

"**S**hit."

Angie Larson pulled into the cemetery as Brother Grover began his opening prayer. The cemetery was small, and she could see the bowed heads from the gate. Rather than make a scene, she parked just inside the gates and hopped out.

"Shit, shit, shit," she murmured. Her sandals slapped the pavement as she trotted across the cemetery. She could hear Grover droning on the closer she got. A late patient at the doctor's office put her behind. She felt bad enough about missing the service, and now she was late to the burial. But, she'd been to a few of Grover's memorial services, and if she'd learned anything, he was just getting started.

"Father, give us compassion in this, our time of mourning. Lay your comforting hands upon us and dry our tears."

Yep, Angie thought, *he's getting wound up.*

"Let us not despair, but instead find peace in the knowledge our beloved Candace is now at your side in the kingdom of Heaven. Oh Lord, shine your light upon us, so we don't walk in the dark."

Oh, boy.

"Spread your touch to each and every one of these people here today. Fill them with your holy spirit like you have filled me."

And there he goes.

Grover held his hands up in the air. Sweat poured down his face. He swayed back and forth, shuffling his feet from side to side.

"I feel you with us now, Lord. Give us your blessings on—"

Grover stepped backward into a dip in the grass. His arms flailed as he tried to find his balance, but momentum forced him down onto his bottom and into a backward somersault. The crowd gasped. He crashed to a halt against a stone in the next row, panting and bewildered.

Angie bit her lip to stifle a smile. A few mourners rushed to the fallen pastor's side. Her dad stood up front with an amused grin on his face. He turned toward the rest of the crowd, saw her standing there fighting the laughter, and winked. Angie turned to the girl standing in the back beside her, who watched on in dazed confusion.

"First time for a Grover service?" Angie asked.

The girl turned to her and nodded. "Yeah, first time."

"Paula?"

"Yeah," Paula answered.

"I'm Angie. Don't know if you remember me or not."

"Yeah, of course."

"It's good to see you," Angie said.

"Same. Uncle Larry said you were coming."

"Yeah, I couldn't get out of work, so I had to miss the service. We'll catch up later. Grover is ready to roll again."

"I think he's rolled enough," Paula said.

Angie snorted laughter, clamping her hand over mouth.

Paula stifled a smile herself.

Grover brought the service to a close without further incident. As the crowd dispersed, people took turns walking up to the casket, taking a flower, patting the lid. Paula held her place, waiting for the area to clear out. Angie stayed by her side.

The crowd diminished until only Angie, Paula, Larry, and Grover remained. Grover shook Larry's hand, nodded at the girls, then trudged away, rubbing the pop knot on his head. Paula approached the gravesite. The stone was already in place. Candace made all her funeral arrangements years ago. It was a soft gray granite that sparkled in the sunlight. An engraving of an angel playing a harp adorned the bottom. Paula gently plucked a pink rose from one of the bouquets on top and held it to her chest.

"I'll miss you," she said. "I'm sorry I didn't come see you more."

Larry stepped up beside her and put a massive arm around her shoulders. "Don't beat yourself up, kid. Candy knew where your heart was."

Paula nodded and leaned into Larry's chest. When she pulled away, a damp spot was left on his suit jacket from her tears. "I've made a mess of you."

Larry looked at the spot and chuckled. "You ain't seen nothing yet, honey. Wait til we get back to the house for dinner. I'll have barbecue sauce all over this thing."

"He will," Angie chimed in. "Dad has to load up his plate with extra food to make up for all the bites he drops on his shirt."

Paula smiled. "Oh, I appreciate the offer, but I don't plan to stay."

"What?" Larry's eyes widened. "You didn't drive all the way down here, just to turn around and go back a couple hours later, did ya?"

"Oh, you have to stay. I haven't seen you since we were little. Do you really have to go?" Angie asked.

Paula hesitated. "I guess I'm not in that big of a rush."

"Thatta girl," Larry said. He beamed a wide smile and motioned for them to follow. "It was the barbecue that did it, wasn't it?"

Paula laughed and walked with them back to the car. A gentle breeze picked up and Paula stopped, turning back toward the gravesite.

"What is it?" Angie asked.

"Do you smell that?"

Angie sniffed. She did smell something. "Smells like honey."

"Honeysuckle perfume," Paula said. She turned to look at Angie and Larry. "Aunt Candace always wore it. That's what it smells like."

Angie's arms broke out in goosebumps.

"There ya go, then," Larry said. "Maybe Candy wanted us to know she's still with us."

"Maybe so," Paula answered. She smiled and followed Larry.

Angie stood still a moment longer. The scent of honeysuckle was still strong. Paula was right. It was exactly like Candy's perfume.

"You comin?" Larry called back.

"Yep," Angie replied. She jogged toward them, pushing the thought of phantom smells from her mind. *Probably some flowers around here,* she thought. The idea of Candy's spirit manifesting the smell of her perfume in a cemetery made her uneasy. *Flowers, that's all.*

CHAPTER 3

Walking into Larry's home was like stepping out of a time machine. Passing through the foyer and into the small kitchen filled Paula with memories long forgotten. Most of the furniture still held its place exactly where it was twenty years before. Even the smell was the same—well water, apples, and cigarette smoke. A jigsaw puzzle lay scattered across the kitchen table. Paula's heart ached at the sight of it. Aunt Candace loved puzzles, and the two of them spent many evenings piecing together horses, flowers, or whatever was in stock at the general store.

"It's easier if you put together the outer edge first, you know?"

Larry turned away from the refrigerator where he was pulling trays of food covered in aluminum foil.

"That's Candy's way. Never cared for it. I group pieces together that look like they match and build out from there. The outside is easy if the inside's already done."

"Fair enough," Paula said, smiling. "Mind if I use your bathroom?"

"Course not. You remember where it is?"

"I think I can find my way."

"I suppose so. Make yourself at home."

"Thanks, Uncle Larry—for everything."

Larry beamed at her. "You're welcome, sweet pea. I'll get the food going."

"Sounds good." Paula left the kitchen and stepped into the living room. Picture frames lined the walls and all available shelf space. She stifled a laugh. Home decoration was definitely not Larry's thing.

Centered on the large mantle was a picture she recognized. Aunt Candace had the same picture hanging in her house. Paula's mother and father stood beside each other with Lonny and Paula posed in front. Larry and his wife Debbie were next, Larry holding baby Angie in his arms, and Candace stood on the end. Paula picked up the frame gently and slid the photo out. Someone had written on the back—**The Tompkins Family: David, Claire, Larry, Debbie, Candy, Lonny, Paula, and Angie.**

Sadness washed over Paula. This was from a time when things were better. A time before death and loneliness and neglect. She put the photo back in the frame and replaced it on the mantle, then scanned the rest of the photos in the room. Some she knew, but most were very old with deep creases and yellowed edges showing people from a time long before her. Several photos featured entire families posed in front of their homes. Very few smiled. The hard life they led was etched on their faces. Even the children looked weary and stoic. The longer she stared into these portals of time, the more uneasy she felt. The cold stares of these relatives from the past chilled the warmth of Angie and Larry's hospitality.

She shivered and hustled through the living room to the short hall, trying to ignore the oppressive feeling of being watched. The bathroom door stood open and she slammed it behind her, more forcefully than she intended. She pressed her back against the door and took steadying breaths. Anxiety was settling in. She fought the panic pressing against her. She counted her breaths—three seconds in, hold for five, exhale for seven. As she struggled to calm her nerves, footsteps thudded out in the hall.

"You okay in there?"

Paula gritted her teeth. "Yeah, sorry. Didn't mean to slam the door."

"Okay. Just checking," Larry called out.

The footsteps retreated, and Paula returned focus to her breathing. She counted through a few more cycles and her heart rate slowed. *Keep it together,* she thought. Her shoulders relaxed and she let out a final long exhale, then crossed the small bathroom to the white porcelain sink. She turned on the faucet and let the cold water run over her hands. The medicine cabinet door was ajar, and orange prescription bottles lined the shelves. Rather than snoop, she gently pressed the cabinet closed and stared at her reflection in the mirror.

She looked tired. Her eyelids drooped and the skin under her eyes was darkening. Worry lines creased her forehead and her lips turned down. She ran her fingers through her hair, tucking a few loose strands behind her ear, then dabbed water on her face. She locked eyes with her image in the mirror. Slowly, the face looking back began to distort. The wall behind her grew dark. The face in the mirror was no longer her own. The corners of the mouth pulled upward in a tight-lipped grin.

Paula gasped and shut her eyes. The faucet hissed, and she fumbled blindly for the handle.. Her fingers found it and twisted it shut.

Get your shit together, girl. You're freaking yourself out.

When she opened her eyes, her usual reflection stared back..

Back to the kitchen. Now.

She pushed open the bathroom door, half expecting some new unsettling occurrence to be waiting for her, but the hall was empty. From the kitchen came the squeak of hinges and Larry's muffled voice. Paula bolted down the hall and through the living room, careful not to make eye contact with any more dead relatives. As she reached the kitchen's threshold, Angie popped into the doorway. Paula tensed and jerked backwards, swallowing the scream in her throat.

"Whoa, sorry 'bout that," Angie said with a chuckle. "Am I that scary?"

Paula sighed and shook her head. "Sorry. I'm just a little on edge. Being back here is...difficult."

Angie gave a sympathetic smile. "Come on. Let's help Dad with the food."

"No you won't," Larry shouted from the kitchen. "I don't need help. You two go sit outside in the shade. I'll holler when it's ready."

Both girls smiled and Angie nodded towards the door.

"Fine, then," Angie said. She led the way back through the kitchen, past Larry who now stood by the counter stirring a tray of baked beans. "If you decide you need help, don't ask us. You already had your chance."

Larry snorted and winked at Paula as she passed by. Already the uneasy feelings from before were fading, and she made a note to not wander off alone any more than she had to. Larry and Angie's presence seemed to ward off the bad feelings waiting to ambush her.

Paula followed Angie outside and across the yard. An old wooden picnic table sat shaded beneath a big oak tree.

"Can I get you something to drink?" Angie asked as they sat down across from each other.

"No, I'm fine," Paula answered.

"We've got some really good lemonade. I'll get you some when dinner's ready."

"Thanks."

"Even better with vodka mixed in," Angie said. "Do you drink?"

"Sometimes. Not a lot."

"Good. We'll sample some of that later, then."

Paula smiled, but she had no intention of drinking alcohol before driving back.

"So, what do you do back home?" Angie asked.

"I work in a factory. We make latex gloves."

"Oh, that sounds cool."

"Really?"

Angie laughed. "No, not really. But a job's a job. If it pays well, and you don't hate it, that's all that matters, right?"

"It keeps my bills paid and a roof on my head. That's enough for me. How about you? Larry said you work at a doctor's office. Are you a nurse?"

"Yeah. It's a small office. I do receptionist work, too. Check people in, run their insurance, collect payments. Real exciting stuff."

"Sounds like a good job to me."

"Yeah, it is. What's Ohio like?"

"It's not a whole lot different than here, actually."

"Really? That's kind of disappointing, isn't it?"

"It feels different, I guess. No mountains, but a lot of countryside. Where I live is mostly farmland. But, the cities are fun. I go to Cincinnati sometimes."

"I've never been. Lexington is the biggest city I've ever been to. I'm so sheltered," Angie said. "We should go to a Reds game together sometime."

"Yeah, that would be fun," Paula said. She was surprised to realize she meant it. It felt good to connect with family again. She hadn't realized how much she missed it.

The screen door squeaked open and Larry leaned out. "Alright, ladies, your feast is ready! Come make a plate and we'll eat there at the picnic table."

Paula followed Angie back into the house. Her stomach rumbled at the smell of barbeque now filling the small kitchen. Aluminum foil trays filled the countertops and the table.

"Wow, you just threw all this together?" Paula asked.

Angie chuckled. "Yeah, dad can't actually cook."

"'Fraid so," Larry said, "but I do a damn fine job heating up trays of food. Been a steady train of folks dropping by to give their condolences, and every one of them brought me something to eat. I'm mighty glad you stayed or else me and Angie would've eaten ourselves into a coma."

"I don't think I'm going to make enough difference to save you."

"I'll feel better knowing you helped us dig through it."

Paula filled her plate with pulled pork, baked beans, mac and cheese, and mashed potatoes, then headed back to the picnic table. Angie carried a pitcher of lemonade and three glasses. They sat and ate, conversation dying to a minimum as they cleared their plates.

The sun drifted lower, skimming the mountain tops to the west. They'd all gone back for seconds, and now the remains of a tray of peach cobbler sat between them on the picnic table.

"Oh lord, I believe I'm about to bust," Larry said. He leaned back and stretched.

"I can't eat another bite," Paula said. "I want to because it's so good, but I can't."

Angie smiled. "That's one good thing about the mountain. Everybody makes good food. Well, except for Dad."

"Thank you both for the hospitality. It means a lot to me. I dreaded coming back here, and you two have made it a lot easier."

"You're not leaving now, are you?" Larry asked. His forehead crinkled. "I don't like the idea of you driving through the mountain and all that way on the interstate after dark. You ought to stay with us for the night."

"I couldn't do that. Really, I already planned on getting home late. It's not a big deal."

"That was before you stayed for dinner," Angie said. "You would've gotten home late if you left right after the burial. If you leave now, it'll be the middle of the night. Stay with us. I like having you around."

Paula smiled. She thought about the relief she would feel to leave the mountain in her rearview again. But, spending time with Larry and Angie had been fun. It felt unexpectedly good to be with family.

"Come on," Angie said. "I told you earlier you have to try this lemonade with a little bit of the special sugar."

Paula sighed. "Okay, fine. I'll stay."

"Good," Larry said. "That makes me feel better. I've got an old fold out cot I can set up in Angie's room. You girls can have a slumber party." He stood and stretched again. "Candy would be so happy to see you two together again. I'd like to think she does see it, too." He nodded, then trudged back toward the house.

Paula watched him go. Dusk had arrived and the crickets were in full chorus. Firefly flashes dotted the yard.

"Well," Angie said. "I'll go get the vodka."

CHAPTER 4

Night came and wrapped the sky in a brilliant blanket of stars. Paula stared up at the shimmering display in awed fascination. She'd forgotten how vivid the sky could be when you were far from the haze of city lights. Somewhere in the distance, a bullfrog croaked.

"Ribbit," Angie said.

Paula had just taken a drink of her spiked lemonade and snorted laughter, shooting it through her nose and sending her into a coughing fit. Angie cackled beside her and slapped her back.

"It burns," Paula said between fits of laughter and wheezing coughs.

The lemonade and a half empty fifth of Smirnoff sat on the table between them. After dinner they'd relocated to two rocking chairs on the back porch. Larry went to bed early.

"This is fun," Angie said. "I'm glad you're here."

Paula smiled. "It is fun. I never thought I'd say it, but I'm glad I'm here, too."

Angie frowned. "Was it that bad? I was pretty young when you left. I don't know what happened."

Paula bit her lip and dropped her head.

"Shit, Paula, I'm sorry. We don't have to talk about it. I shouldn't have brought it up."

"No, it's fine. I'm just drunk enough to let it out. Maybe that's a good thing."

"Are you sure? Seriously, don't drudge up bad shit because I opened my mouth."

"I think I need to talk about it. I've spent all these years trying to forget, but things don't just go away." Paula turned to Angie and cocked an eyebrow. "You up for being my therapist?"

Angie chuckled and took a swig from her glass. "Blind leading the blind there, but why not. We'll do it together."

"It wasn't always bad. Things didn't go to shit until after Mother died. Before that, I remember things being okay. I have happy memories. Things weren't roses, but they were better. We didn't have much, but nobody around here did. We had what we needed. Daddy was different then. I can't explain it. He was never a happy-go-lucky kind of guy, but he took care of us. Lonny was a few years older than me, and he helped Daddy with the chores. You probably don't remember Lonny at all, do you?"

Angie shook her head.

"No, you were too young when that happened. Anyway, yeah, Lonny was pretty close to Daddy, stayed by his side most of the time. And I was with Mother. Normal life. If Mother wouldn't have gotten sick, things might have been very different. I used to think about that all the time. Daydreaming about what things would have been like if Mother would've lived."

"How old were you when she got sick?"

"Eleven. Well, it turned out she was sick long before that, but we didn't know. I was eleven when we found out. Twelve when she died."

"Damn."

"Yeah. Damn. That's a shitty time to lose your mom, too, ya know? A twelve year old girl. Lot of things happening around then that it'd be nice to talk to your mom about."

"I can't imagine," Angie said. She sipped the last drink from her cup then went to refill it. The pitcher quivered in her hand and she squinted at it while she poured. "My mom was a flake, but at least she stuck around long enough to teach me a few things."

"You ever see her?"

"Not really. We haven't talked in a long time. I see her around, but I make sure she doesn't see me. Been down that road enough times to know where it ends."

"Where's that?"

"With her asking me for money."

"Yuck."

"Yeah. I wouldn't mind helping her out if that's what I was doing. But it's not. You give her money, she gives it to the bar. Round and round we go."

Paula nodded. She thought of Larry asleep inside and how unfair it was that his wife ended up a deadbeat alcoholic. She remembered things going south with their marriage right before she left the mountains. Aunt Candance filled her in on the details later.

"Good thing we both had Aunt Candace."

"Absolutely. She was a great woman." Angie held her glass up in a toast. "May she rest in peace."

Paula lifted her glass and clinked it against Angie's.

"So, then Mother got sick and she didn't get better. Even before she passed, Daddy started taking off on us. Couldn't even wait for her to be gone. We'd be there for days and never see him at all. Me and Lonny took care of her the best we could."

"Maybe he just couldn't deal with it?"

"That's the kind of thing you *have* to deal with. It was sad and awful, but it was happening, and giving your children no choice but to deal with it while you run around was a dick move. That's where the bad feelings started for me. He didn't support us. We might as well have been orphans."

"I'm sorry."

"Yeah, me too," Paula said. She downed her drink and poured herself a fresh glass, hands shaking.

Angie noticed and gently took the pitcher from her and finished pouring. "Let's talk about something else. I think we've had enough time down this memory lane."

Paula smiled and nodded. Her eyelids drooped as the alcohol surged through her. "What's next on our slumber party agenda?"

"We don't know the same boys, so that's boring," Angie said. "Oh, I know, how about we tell ghost stories?"

"Yes!" Paula shouted then burst into laughter. "We should go on a haunted adventure. What are the good ghost spots around here?"

"Ghost spots?"

"You know, like every town has a Cry Baby Bridge or a creepy old house where all the murders happened."

"Well, we're definitely not driving anywhere," Angie said. Her face grew serious and she eyed Paula. "You remember the stories about King's Creek Cemetery?"

"Hmm." Paula's brow knitted as she combed through memories. "Nope, doesn't ring a bell."

"Really?" Angie's eyes widened. "I thought everybody knew about that place."

"Where is it?"

"About a mile from here, and you can walk there. There's a trail through the woods back there that'll dump you out close to it," Angie said pointing toward the trees.

"What's the story?" Paula asked.

Angie sipped her lemonade. "Weird shit, ghosts and witches and stuff like that." She looked down at the ground. "I saw something there once when I was young."

"No shit! Tell me."

"I was out playing in the woods back there, not too far from the house, but it was November, and the leaves had fallen. I was making big piles and jumping into them. You ever do that?"

Paula nodded. The thought triggered memories and she could smell the damp, sweet smell of the leaves, hear the crunch as she dove into piles.

"Like I said, the cemetery's only like a mile away and when the leaves are gone, you can kind of see it. This was after the time changed, so it was already getting dark at like five."

"That's so dumb," Paula said. "Daylight savings time is stupid."

"So, it's getting pretty dark and I'm about to go back home when I see it. Off in the distance there's an orange glow and weird shadows moving around. Curiosity killed the cat, you know, so I go marching further into the woods toward the light. I climbed up this little hill, and from the top, I could see the cemetery."

Angie paused her story and took a long drink.

"Oh, dramatic pause," Paula teased. "What'd you see?"

Angie stared at Paula. Her face was strange.

"What was it?" Paula asked.

"There was a huge fire in the cemetery. It looked like one of the trees was burning. And there were people dancing around it. They looked like shadows, and I couldn't make any of them out, but there were a lot. And, there was—*something* in the fire."

Paula stared back at Angie, genuinely fascinated. "What was in the fire?"

"I don't know, but it looked like a person."

"Like someone was burning in the fire?"

"No," Angie said, wringing her hands. "It was more like the fire was *becoming* a person. And it was looking at me."

Paula leaned back in her chair, shook her head, and took another drink. "What'd you do?"

"It scared the shit out of me. I ran as fast as I could until I hit our back door. Dad was coming around the house, and I got a good ass chewing. He'd been looking for me, and when he couldn't find me, he panicked."

"Damn, girl. That's a good story. Gave me goosebumps. You ever see anything like that again?"

"Never went back to give myself a chance to see it again. I had nightmares for weeks. Kept seeing those people dancing and the thing in the fire."

"We totally have to go," Paula said. She stood up, immediately lost her balance, and stumbled off the porch. She grabbed the wrought-iron support rail and stayed on her feet.

Angie laughed, but there was worry in her eyes. "I don't think you need to be walking anywhere."

"I'm good," Paula said. She dramatically walked a straight line then touched the tip of her nose. "See? Street legal."

"I don't know," Angie said.

"You scared?"

"Maybe a little bit, yeah."

"We'll be together this time," Paula said. "Never leave each other's side. How about that?"

Angie let out a sigh but smiled. "Okay, fine. But if we see some shit that gives me nightmares again, I'm gonna be so mad at you." She stood and gently opened the back screen door. Even from across the house, she heard the steady rumble of snores coming from Larry's bedroom. "The coast is clear."

Paula chuckled. "You're too old to get in trouble for sneaking out. You're a grown ass woman."

"You don't know my dad, then."

"Fair enough," Paula said. "Let's do this."

Angie led the way across the yard, past the picnic table, to the tree line.

"Shit, it's dark."

"Oh yeah," Angie said, then fell into another fit of laughter. "Hold on." She ran back across the yard and disappeared into the house. A moment later, she emerged and a beam of yellow light bounced across the yard as she jogged back to Paula.

"Okay, here goes nothing," Angie said.

She pointed the flashlight into the trees and they disappeared into the dark.

CHAPTER 5

Larry woke to the screen door bouncing off the frame. A quiet hiss of frustration from the kitchen was followed by rustling and then a soft knock he recognized as a drawer closing. He turned and squinted at the glowing red digits on his nightstand clock. It was nearly two in the morning. He smiled and shook his head.

The screen door squeaked and closed again, and he pushed himself out of bed, to the window looking out over the back yard. He saw Angie jogging in zig zag lines across the yard with the flashlight beam bouncing in front of her. In the distance, Paula stood by the tree line at the edge of the property.

What in the hell are those two girls up to?

For a moment he considered pulling up the window and shouting after them, but changed his mind. They were grown women. If they wanted to take a nighttime hike through the woods, who was he to stop them? It'd been far too long since Paula and Angie were together, and he wasn't about to spoil their fun. After the day's events, they could use a good time. He watched them step into the gloom of the trees, and the flashlight beam disappeared, swallowed by dense foliage.

I hope they don't run into any bears or copperheads.

He thought once to lay back down, but knew he wouldn't sleep a wink until the girls returned. With a sigh, he slipped on his leather house shoes and shuffled down the hall. The place was silent aside from the grandfather clock's echoing *tick* in the living room. He passed into the kitchen and poured himself a glass of water, then sat at the table. From here, he had a clear view of the back yard. A half-full pitcher of lemonade and a nearly-empty bottle of vodka sat on the small table between the two chairs on the porch.

Oh lord, he thought. Uneasiness gripped him. Those two girls were three sheets to the wind, and he now regretted not trying to stop them wandering off. At least they were together. He sipped his water. Who would've thought after all these years, he'd be sitting up waiting for Angie and Paula to come back from a drunken late night hike? He chuckled in spite of himself.

Larry always thought fondly of Paula. His heart sank when he remembered what she'd endured growing up on the mountain. Losing her mama, then losing Lonny in the accident. It was hard for everyone, and David didn't make it any easier. He should've been there for those kids when Claire passed. Instead, he was out running around. It got worse when Lonny died. Larry spent many nights trying to talk sense into his brother, but by then David was too far gone. He was deep in the drink and looked sick all the time, but there was a fierceness to him Larry never knew before. They'd grown up thick as thieves, close as brothers could be. Losing your wife was hard. Larry knew from experience, albeit a different set of circumstances, but Debbie was lost to him all the same. He knew how much it hurt, but it didn't justify abandoning your family. There were many times he'd gone to get Lonny and little Paula because he knew they'd been home alone for too long. He'd bring them home with him, but Debbie struggled to manage Angie and adding two more to the mix would send her over the edge every time. So, usually he'd take them to Candy. She became a mom to them, something he thought Claire would've been thankful for.

After Paula turned eighteen and hightailed it out of the mountain, David became a total recluse. Larry tried to reason with him, but never had any success. The few times Larry could track him down, what he found was a shell of a man with no trace of the brother he remembered. So much bad history lay in these hills. Claire and Lonny dying like they did, Debbie leaving him and marrying the bottle, David losing everything and chasing God knows what. He didn't blame Paula one bit for getting out. He'd be lying if he said the thought hadn't crossed his mind many times. But, this was still home to him, and he supposed it always would be. Someone had to carry the torch.

He stood and crossed the kitchen, then stepped out onto the back porch. It was still warm, but the humidity had broken. He strained to listen for any sound of the girls. If they were as drunk as he figured they were, they'd have a hell of a time being quiet. The night was silent except for the cricket songs and the occasional bullfrog.

Come on, girls. Don't get yourselves into trouble. I'm too old to go on a search and rescue.

He paced, listening for branches moving or sticks snapping underfoot. Anything to reassure him the girls were okay. There wasn't much out there to see, anyway. What were they looking for? He pondered the question, then stopped abruptly.

That damned cemetery.

His stomach dropped. Angie would never go there on her own, especially not at night. He vividly remembered the nightmares she had about the place as a child—the screams jolting him from sleep. His eyes fell on the table and the pitcher of what Angie called "Lightning Lemonade". Liquid courage is what it was. Couple that with safety in numbers and a sense of adventure, and it all made sense. Larry cursed himself for not trying to stop them when he had the chance.

His instincts told him to go after them and bring them home, but he resisted. They were grown women. Can't watch them all the time. He frowned, then turned to go back inside and brew some coffee. He got the feeling he probably wasn't going to sleep for a while. His fingers wrapped around the door handle, and he pulled the door open a couple inches then froze. A bloodcurdling scream shattered the night's silence. It was a scream he'd heard many times, though not in years. The voice was deeper now, but he'd know it anywhere.

Somewhere in the trees, Angie shrieked again.

CHAPTER 6

"I really have to pee," Paula said.

"I do, too," Angie replied, "but I'll wait 'til we get back. I'm not taking a chance getting bit in the ass by a snake."

Paula laughed then groaned. "Oh, don't make me laugh. It makes it worse."

Angie smiled. This was the most fun she'd had in years. As scared as she was to revisit the cemetery that haunted her dreams as a child, it was exhilarating to be out here with Paula. She felt a connection between them and tried not to think about Paula leaving tomorrow.

The remnants of a trail was barely visible. At one time it'd been maintained, but over the years the forest took it back. Angie kept the flashlight beam focused on the narrow line of dirt in front of her so she wouldn't lose the path. The swishing weeds and crunching twigs meant Paula was still behind her.

"How far did you say it is?" Paula asked.

"About a mile, probably. Maybe a little less. It's hard to tell through the woods. The path curves a lot. If you could go in a straight line, it's probably only half a mile."

"As the crow flies," Paula said.

Angie smiled. "That's right. As the crow flies. Aunt Candy used to say that all the time."

"You think she's watching us?"

"I hope not," Angie replied. "She wouldn't want us out here like this. She'd tell us to stop being foolish. That's another thing she used to say all the time. Don't be foolish."

"Yep. She used that one on me quite a few times."

They marched on in silence. Angie tried not to let her mind wander. As much as she fought against it, she could feel the trees closing in around her. The further they got from the house, the heavier the air felt. Images of that night flashed in her mind. The fire, the figures, the shouting. With each step, she became more convinced this was not a good idea. Doom clouded her mind. Paula's voice broke through her thoughts.

"What's that?"

Angie stopped and turned. Paula pointed up ahead.

"You see it?"

Angie's blood went cold. The landscape ahead steadily rose to a crest blocking the view of anything past it, but the sky visible through the trees had an orange hue.

"Is that a fire?"

Angie's heart pounded, and suddenly she was a little girl again.

"Holy shit," Paula exclaimed. "That's a fire. It's flickering. Do you see?" Paula grabbed Angie's arm and shook it.

Angie locked eyes with Paula, and the excitement melted from Paula's face.

"Hey, it's okay. I'm here. You're not alone. You're not a little girl out here by yourself."

Angie clenched her jaw and nodded.

"We can go back if you want."

Every instinct in her body screamed at her to say yes and go back home, but already the glimmer in Paula's eyes was returning, and Angie didn't want to disappoint her.

"Let's keep going. I want to see," Angie lied.

"Just a peek," Paula said. "We'll climb up and stay low in case there's something weird happening, and then we'll go back."

"Yeah," Angie said. "Just a peek."

"Turn off the flashlight," Paula said. "We're sneaking."

Angie clicked off the light and shoved it in her pocket.

Paula grabbed her hand and they walked cautiously up the incline. Once, Angie's foot got tangled in a root and she nearly screamed. Paula managed to pull her up and keep them both from crashing to the ground.

"Careful," Paula whispered. "You good?"

Angie nodded and they continued. As they reached the top, they squatted low and slid down onto their stomachs, shimmying up until their heads popped over the crest. Neither spoke.

The cemetery in the valley below was small, entirely visible from their high-ground perspective. A massive tree marked the center. Under normal circumstances, the tree added a scenic beauty to an otherwise melancholy locale. There was nothing beautiful about it now.

The tree was on fire.

Flames swirled through the branches and lashed out at the sky. The orange glow spread in all directions, expanding even beyond the cemetery's boundaries. A crackling sound filled the air.

"Oh my God," Paula whispered.

Angie couldn't speak. Her muscles were locked tight and her hands shook, fingers tensed into claws digging into the dirt.

"There's no smoke," Paula said. She turned to Angie. "What the hell is this?"

Angie fought against her paralyzing fear and tried to comprehend what Paula said. She stared at the burning tree and realized Paula was right. No smoke rose into the air. She inhaled deeply. No smell of burning wood or leaves either. The flames crawled through the branches with unnatural slowness. The colors were wrong. Everything was wrong.

"This is weird, Angie. Look at how the—" Paula's voice froze mid-sentence.

Paula's eyes were locked on the cemetery. She slowly lifted a hand and pointed. Angie gasped.

One by one, black figures rose from the ground around the burning tree. Angie realized they'd been there all along, kneeling, unmoving. When the last of the figures stood, they all swayed, arms outstretched to the flaming night.

"Fuck this," Paula whispered. "Time to go."

Paula's hand clamped down on Angie's wrist and she stood, pulling Angie up with her. As they turned to leave, Paula put a finger to her mouth, signaling Angie to be quiet. Angie nodded, then froze. Quiet. A sickening dread fell over her. It *is* quiet. Too quiet.

As if Angie's thought had been transferred via telepathy, Paula's eyes widened. The girls turned slowly back to the valley below.

In the cemetery, the figures stood motionless, staring up the hill in silence broken only by the crackling fire. One figure lifted a hand and pointed directly at the girls. Instantly, the fire vanished and the forest collapsed into utter darkness.

Angie could hold it back no longer, and her scream split the night.

CHAPTER 7

Paula flinched at the piercing scream. The sudden loss of light left her disoriented. She blinked, desperate to clear her vision. Angie screamed again, and Paula pulled her close and clamped a hand over her mouth, stifling a third. She focused on the ground in front of them, blinking and squinting the landscape into view. Behind them, limbs and bushes rattled and snapped. Her blood ran cold. Those people were coming up the hill.

"Run," Paula hissed, then took off down the incline, praying to stay on her feet. Angie raced along beside her, their hands still locked together. She whimpered as she ran, but thankfully didn't scream again. They reached the bottom unscathed and pressed on into the trees. The path seemed more narrow than before. Tree branches hanging above their heads previously now reached toward the ground, steering them into thicker brush.

"I can't see the trail," Paula whispered.

Angie whimpered.

I can't see. Why can't I see?

"Where's the flashlight?"

Angie stopped and stared at Paula in confusion. Her body trembled.

Paula grabbed her by the shoulders. "Flashlight, Angie. Where is it?"

Another branch snapped in the woods behind them, accompanied by a soft giggle.

Angie heard it, too, and her eyes widened even more.

"Angie, I don't know the way out. Where is the flashlight? Help me."

The pleading tone in her voice finally registered, and Angie reached into her pocket, pulling the flashlight free. She snapped it on and the beam illuminated the trees to their left. Angie shrieked again. Paula let out a wail of her own.

An ancient, weathered face stared at them from the foliage. The skin was so wrinkled and dry it blended with the tree bark beside it. Were it not for the yellow eyes reflecting the light, Paula might not have seen it at all. The face smiled, a hideous gesture revealing broken teeth and a pale tongue coiled out, flicking at the air. With fingers far too long, it raked jagged nails down the tree trunk, leaving deep grooves.

Paula yanked Angie backward, and the face disappeared from view. Angie led them in the other direction. The flashlight beam bounced from side to side, but Paula didn't dare follow it. She didn't want to see that face again. She kept her eyes locked on Angie's feet and chased after her, step for step.

The face in the trees had replaced Angie's hysteria with a dogged determination to escape. The roles were now reversed and Paula was grateful to hand over the reins.

Whispers and cackles sounded in the dark around them, coming from all directions. Paula gritted her teeth against the urge to scream, keeping her hand locked around Angie's. She knew in her heart if they separated, the forest would take them, and she'd never leave this place again. A large tree crashed to the ground, sending birds and other night creatures into a frenzy. Whispering and crunching assaulted her ears.

Angie zig-zagged through trees, leaping over vines and logs. Paula saw no sign of the trail and desperately hoped Angie knew where she was going. Branches thrashed and dark shadows skated just beyond her view, but she kept her eyes forward and down. Something grabbed her shirt and pulled. She shrieked and twisted forward. Fabric ripped, and the pressure was gone. She tried to convince herself it was a low hanging branch that caught her shirt, but the icy touch on her back told her otherwise.

"ANGIE!"

Both girls looked toward the call. Relief washed over Paula. It was Larry. He was close.

Angie banked hard to the right. Light filtered through the trees ahead. The sounds of pursuit quieted, then stopped altogether. The trail appeared below them and the trees opened up. A huge shadow filled the opening and Paula almost screamed, but then Larry's voice came again.

"GIRLS!"

They burst out of the trees, Angie into Larry's arms and Paula onto the ground. Angie wept and clung desperately to her father. Paula pushed herself up onto her elbows and stared into the trees. All was quiet, but deep in the woods, she swore she caught a glimpse of yellow eyes peering back at her.

"What the hell is going on here?" Larry asked. He gently pushed Angie away from him, keeping his hands on her shoulders. "Angie, talk to me. What happened?"

Angie attempted to speak, then collapsed into more sobs, burying her face into his shoulder. Larry pulled her into his arms. He turned to Paula, still laying on the ground.

Paula stared back, but found herself unable to speak. Instead, she shook her head.

Larry held her gaze for a moment, nodded, then guided Angie back across the lawn toward the house. "Let's get you girls inside."

Paula climbed to her feet and followed them. Larry pulled open the screen door and squeezed through the opening with Angie still pressed against him. Paula gave one last look back at the woods. Nothing moved and the trees were dark, but she could feel eyes on her. In the distance, someone or *something* laughed.

CHAPTER 8

Larry stood by the counter and watched the girls. The smell of freshly brewed coffee filled the kitchen. Each of them had a cup. Larry sipped his in silence. He'd told the girls to take a few minutes and compose themselves, hoping the caffeine would sober them up enough to explain what the hell happened. Angie was no longer crying, and the shaking in her hands was fading. Paula sat motionless, staring out the window with a grim expression. The tension eased with each tick of the grandfather clock. The coffee and bright lights seemed to calm their nerves.

"So, you two want to tell me what happened out there? You run into a bear?"

Angie shook her head. Paula said nothing.

"Okay, then what was it?"

Angie stuttered and stumbled over words, trying to put together a sentence, but failed. Paula made no effort to help explain. Larry eyed her with concern. She seemed *off*.

"Paula," Larry said, "could you help me out here and explain what happened?"

"You won't believe it," Paula said flatly.

"Why do you think that?"

"Because I don't believe it, either."

"Well, let me be the judge, then. Start with what you two were doing out there to begin with."

Paula sighed. "We were talking about old times, telling stories, and Angie told me about a cemetery in the woods that freaked her out when she was little."

"King's Creek Cemetery," Larry said. A chill ran up his spine as he said the words. *That damned place.*

"Yeah, I think so. We were feeling good, had a few drinks, and it sounded like a fun idea to go explore."

"I assume Angie told you about her *experience* there. Did she tell you how she had nightmares for months?"

"Yes," Paula said. "It was stupid to go out there. She didn't want to, but I pushed her into it."

"No," Angie said, speaking clearly for the first time. "You didn't make me go. I could've said no. We were drunk and it sounded fun."

Larry groaned and shook his head. "Okay, then. You went out to the cemetery to poke around, and then what happened?"

"It happened again," Angie said, her voice barely a whisper.

"What happened again?"

"All of it." Angie's eyes glistened with tears. "The fire, the shapes, the people...all of it."

Larry kept his eyes locked on Angie's.

"Paula, did you see this, too?"

Paula didn't respond immediately. Angie turned toward her, eyes wide.

"Tell him, Paula."

"Yeah, we saw a fire, and people were in the cemetery. I guess. That's what it looked like, but maybe we imagined it."

Angie looked like she'd been slapped.

"Imagined it?" Angie shouted.

"How could that have been real?" Paula asked. She took Angie's hands from across the table. "We were both drunk. It was dark. You told the story from when you were a kid. We were totally primed to freak ourselves out."

"What about when the fire went out? What about the—*face*?"

Larry twitched. "What face?"

"Angie, that was a trick of the light."

"What face?" Larry repeated.

"When we were running back to the house we got lost," Angie said. "I'd forgotten about the flashlight until she reminded me. When I turned it on there was a face in the trees. It was awful. It had yellow eyes and a long tongue like a snake."

Larry kept his face neutral. Internally, his stomach twisted in knots. Memories of years past flooded his mind, things he'd buried for a long time.

"I was scared to death, Angie," Paula said, "but this couldn't be real. I don't believe in ghosts and monsters in the woods. We had too much to drink and let ourselves get wrapped up in our own imaginations."

Angie huffed. "If it was our imagination, then how did we see the same thing?"

Paula started to reply, then stopped and grimaced.

Angie returned her attention to Larry. "Do you believe me, Dad?"

Larry dropped his head and sighed. He was torn. Agreeing with Paula and laying blame to alcohol and the power of suggestion appealed to his need to comfort them. But that would be a lie. He believed every word of Angie's story. He decided to toe the line and stay neutral.

"I believe you think you saw something out there. I wasn't with you, so I can't say if it was real or a wound up imagination, but I know you're both scared and tired, and you need to rest."

Angie's shoulders slumped. Paula seemed satisfied with his answer and nodded.

"Why don't you two go on to bed and try to sleep. I know you just drank coffee, but I think between the alcohol and the excitement, that oughta be enough to knock you out soon enough. We'll talk about it tomorrow when we have the good sense of the sun to help us see."

Angie stood without a word and led the way out of the kitchen. Paula rose from her chair and followed. She paused briefly and patted Larry on the shoulder.

"I'm sorry," she said softly. "She won't admit it, but I pushed her to go out there. I should've known better."

"It's alright," Larry said. "Go get some rest."

Paula disappeared into the living room.

Larry stood in the kitchen, listening to the footsteps fade down the hall and the soft thud of the bedroom door closing. He exhaled and ran a hand over his head. Slowly, he walked to the back door and stepped outside. The usual night sounds greeted him. Nothing seemed out of place or unusual. He scanned the tree line, and saw nothing but shadows.

King's Creek Cemetery.

Why'd they have to go there?

He thought about the face Angie described. Yellow eyes and a snake's tongue. She hadn't said it, but he also knew about the razor sharp teeth and the cracked, dry skin. He'd never seen it himself, thank God, but he'd been told about it. He didn't believe it then, at least not right away. There were plenty of reasons to doubt the source. After everything that happened, he'd had no choice but to believe. Even so, he'd buried those memories deep. The alternative was madness. Angie's words stirred dread in his heart.

Sweet Jesus, he thought, *don't let it happen again.*

CHAPTER 9

Angie woke to muffled voices in the house. She squinted against the broken beams of sunlight cascading through the window blinds. Her head throbbed and her stomach churned. The light was daggers to her eyes and she groaned, pulling the pillow over her face.

As she fought against the hangover nausea, last night's events flooded back. In the cold morning light, it seemed like a bad dream. Already, the burning tree, the dancing figures, and that awful face were losing clarity. The logical part of her brain bucked against her memories. She hadn't believed it then, but her father's words made more sense with every passing second.

We were drunk and amped up, looking for a scare. That's all it was. Imaginations running wild.

But she still struggled against this rationalization. She'd been drunk before, and she'd been in those woods before. The idea that all the things they saw had been imagined was a tough pill to swallow.

With a groaning sigh, she sat up and dropped her feet onto the floor. The room spun and her stomach clenched in response. She took steadying breaths, then stood and crossed the hall to the bathroom. After relieving herself, she splashed cold water on her face. That helped. She dried her hands and made for the kitchen.

The house was silent, and the kitchen was empty. Also missing was the breakfast spread she expected to find. Larry loved breakfast food and never missed an opportunity to indulge. It was odd to see only a couple coffee mugs on the table. Frowning, she went to the back door and stepped out.

Larry stood outside, beyond the porch. Paula stood by her car. She now wore faded jeans and a t-shirt Angie recognized from deep in her own closet.

Larry turned and nodded. "Morning, Sunshine."

Angie patted his arm, then waved at Paula.

"I like your outfit," Angie said.

Paula smiled. "It fits me just right. I hope you don't mind. After our adventure last night, my funeral dress was pretty gross."

"I figured you wouldn't miss them," Larry chimed in.

"Not at all, keep them. A souvenir from our reunion."

"I'll cherish them forever," Paula said.

"You weren't going to leave without saying goodbye, were you?"

"I didn't want to, but I do have to get back, and I didn't want to wake you up. You were snoring so peacefully."

Larry snorted laughter.

Angie slapped his arm. "I get it from my dad."

Larry walked across the yard and embraced Paula.

"I sure am glad you came down. It was damn good to see you again, and I know Candy would be pleased that you came."

"I'm glad I came, too," Paula said. "Thank you again for having me. I wasn't expecting hospitality, to be honest, and you've made me feel welcome."

"Good," Larry said. "Glad to hear it, and you're welcome here any time. Don't wait for me to kick the bucket before you come back."

"I won't," Paula replied.

"Be safe on the road, and if you'd humor an old man, give me a call and let me know you made it back in one piece."

"Sure thing," Paula said, then gave him one more hug.

"I'll let you two have a minute. Take care of yourself, sweet pea."

Angie stepped aside and let Larry pass through the screen door.

She was overcome with emotions; joy at spending time with Paula, sadness that she was leaving so soon, and unease from the experiences they shared in the woods. She cast a glance toward the trees. They looked like they always did.

"Interesting night," Paula said.

"You could say that."

"You're dad's right, you know. What we saw, or what we *thought* we saw, none of that could be real."

"It felt pretty damn real at the time, but, yeah."

"Maybe we stumbled on some people having a bonfire, and then let our imaginations run wild?"

Angie nodded. "Maybe."

"One thing I know for sure," Paula said, "I think I'm good on lemonade and vodka for a while."

Angie chuckled. "Same."

Paula walked over and gave her a quick hug. "I'm really glad I got to hang out with you again. It's been a long time since I've had so much fun, all things considered."

"Me too," Angie said. A lump grew in her throat and she tried to laugh it off. "You're gonna make me cry."

"That's okay, me, too."

"Is it okay if I call you sometime? Maybe we can get together every now and then?"

"You better. I used to meet Candy halfway and we'd have lunch or dinner. Let's do that soon."

"Awesome. Well, I guess I'll let you get on the road."

"Yep, I need to get a move on." Paula walked back to her car and pulled open the door, then turned back. "Call me, Angie. I mean it. Stay in touch. And stay out of the woods." Paula smiled, but her eyes were dead serious.

"Oh, don't worry about that. You wouldn't catch me out there for a million dollars."

Paula nodded, then sat and closed the door. She waved out the window, then pulled away. Angie watched her go until the car disappeared around the curve.

With a sigh, she returned to the back door and stepped inside the kitchen. Larry sat at the table, a fresh cup of coffee steaming in front of him.

"You okay, Dad?"

"I think so," he answered. "Are you okay?"

"I think so." She poured herself a cup then leaned against the counter. "You must be right, about that stuff last night. Had to be our imaginations."

Larry sipped his coffee and stared back at her for a moment.

"Right?" Angie asked.

"Right," Larry finally responded. He held her gaze for another moment, then returned to his coffee. "Nothing out there to worry about. Nothing at all."

CHAPTER 10

The miles crawled by. Paula managed to keep her composure while saying goodbye to Larry and Angie, but inside, she was screaming to leave. The things they saw in the woods weighed on her mind, impossible as they were. She couldn't imagine having to go to bed every night with those memories right across the yard. Her heart broke for Angie. Paula couldn't get away from the mountain fast enough, and ever since merging onto I-75 she'd kept the accelerator mashed to the floor, pushing the old Buick to its limits. Only when the hills in the rearview mirror leveled out and disappeared did she feel even the slightest relief. Now, the mountains were far behind her, and a water tower proudly proclaiming FLORENCE Y'ALL stood ahead in the distance. Florence meant she wasn't far from the sweeping Cincinnati skyline and putting the Ohio River between her and new memories she wanted to forget.

Paula was furious at herself for pushing Angie to go exploring. Up to that point, she was having a great time. Angie was great and spending such a short time with her filled Paula with regret. She didn't regret leaving the holler, not at all. But, she did regret not having a relationship with Angie. Larry, too. It frustrated her to experience what *could* have been if her home life hadn't been so fucked up. She'd gone to the funeral expecting to be in and out—pay her respects and go. Instead she found herself mourning more than Aunt Candy's death, but also a life that could have been.

As Cincinnati came into view along with the bridge that would take her back to Ohio, she burst into tears. It hit like a tidal wave, sobs so deep they strained her back. Tears flooded her eyes and she struggled to see the road. She took the exit to Covington. Ohio would have to wait.

She sat through a couple stop lights, staring straight ahead, not wanting to acknowledge any other drivers who might notice the crying woman. Ahead, she saw a parking area by the river. She needed to get out of the car and collect herself. The lot was empty and, as far as she could see, the bank was free of people as well.

Paula parked and pushed the door open. The sobs lessened, but tears still rolled off her cheeks. A brisk walk along the bank would do her good. The air was warm, and a breeze swept through from the west. It felt good on her skin, and already the tension eased. She sucked in deep breaths, not caring that the air was seasoned with a dank, fishy stench from the river.

Paula wasn't sure if she was having panic attacks or anxiety attacks, or if there was even a difference between the two. What she knew for sure was they were happening more often. She thought of the incident in Larry's living room, when the faces in the picture frames seemed to come alive, how her own reflection in the mirror was different, menacing. *Might be time to see a doctor,* she thought as she walked along the water's edge. She knew she wouldn't. That road went two ways—therapy or pills. Therapy did not appeal to her. It took considerable amounts of alcohol to get her to open up to Angie. In hindsight, it felt good to get things off her chest, but those feelings were overshadowed by the events that followed. Medication was scary. She'd read too many articles about permanent damage and crippling side effects. She had enough problems already without adding chemically induced ones.

A horn sounded in the distance, and Paula looked up the river. A barge floated towards the city. She slowed for a moment and admired the sight.

"It's beautiful, isn't it?"

Paula jerked at the voice and spun. An old man stood several yards behind her. He wore a dingy flannel jacket over a Harley Davidson t-shirt and jeans so caked with dirt they would stand up on their own. His beard was a black with widening gray thatches throughout, tangled and bushy. He wore a red trucker cap nestled on greasy hair that matched his beard.

"The river. It's beautiful, wouldn't you say?"

Paula tensed but tried to keep a calm exterior. He was clearly homeless, and likely harmless, but his abrupt arrival and disheveled appearance had her on edge. "Yes, it is."

"Did I startle you?" the man asked. His voice was surprisingly high pitched. "You look ready to jump out of your skin."

"A little bit," Paula said, laughing nervously. "I didn't see you."

"Most people don't."

"I was just getting some air and stretching my legs. I need to get back on the road."

"Where you headed?"

"Home," Paula said. She took a few steps back the way she came. She took her eyes off the man for a split second to see how far from the car she'd wandered. *Shit,* she thought. She was much farther than she hoped. The car was barely visible, an easy quarter mile away.

"Where've you been?"

"A funeral," Paula replied.

"Oh no," the man replied. "I'm sorry to hear that. Someone close?"

"Yes, my aunt."

"Very sad. Aunts can be as good as mothers, wouldn't you say?"

"Yes."

"You lost your mother, didn't you?"

"I'm sorry, but I have to get going." Paula took a few more steps away from the man.

"You'll be going back, you know?"

"Back where?" She took a few more steps.

"To King's Creek, of course."

Paula froze. "What did you say?"

The man chuckled. "King's Creek. The cemetery."

"Who are you? How do you know that name?"

"Your mother is there, yes?"

"No," Paula said. "My mother's not buried there."

"I didn't say *buried* there."

Paula stared back at the man, unable to move her feet.

"She's there," the man said. He smiled, and his eyes widened. "She's in the fire, waiting for you."

A blast of the barge horn sounded, much closer this time, snapping Paula's attention away from the man. She turned quickly to the river. The barge pulled even with her on the bank, but that was not what held her gaze. In the water, off the bank's edge, what appeared to be a pale, white snake jutted out of the water, wriggling a few inches above the surface. Paula gagged, repulsed by the squiggly meat. Then, the water rippled and a face broke the surface.

It wasn't a snake. It was a tongue. The face rolled forward, letting the tongue slap back into the water, leaving only matted black hair and yellow eyes peeking over the surface.

Paula shrieked and ran.

"They're all waiting for you at King's Creek," the man called out. "You'll be going back soon enough. They're all waiting."

Paula screamed back and pushed herself faster. She closed in quickly on the car, frantically digging the keys from her pocket as she approached. She flung open the door and dove inside, ramming the keys into the ignition. The engine roared to life and she looked back the way she'd come. There was no one in sight. A desperate moan escaped her, and she threw the car in reverse. As she pulled the car back onto the road, she looked in the rearview mirror, but saw nothing save the barge floating down the river. Tears filled her eyes again, and she left the lot the same way she arrived, sobbing uncontrollably.

I'm losing my mind.

CHAPTER 11

Larry sat on the back porch and listened to the rain. His eyes studied the trees, and his foot bounced nervously. Two days had passed since the funeral. Two nights since Paula and Angie went traipsing through the woods. Angie was working at the doctor's office and wouldn't be home until after five. He had the house to himself, but he didn't feel alone.

Ever since Paula left, Larry felt watched. An energy permeated the air, no matter if he was inside or outside. He didn't know a whole lot about science, but he found himself picturing particles buzzing in a space previously at rest. He was constantly uneasy, never able to get comfortable, moving from chair to chair and pacing around the house. With every ounce of his being he hoped things would settle down, but his heart knew otherwise.

It was awake.

The girls stirred up things he'd hoped were gone forever, and it scared him to death. Things were happening, things he convinced himself were not real, and he knew the time was coming when he would have to tell what he knew.

It was easy to be angry at the girls—at Paula particularly—for going out there. Angie knew better, and never would have done that on her own. But, he couldn't stay mad. Paula was a sweet girl, and she couldn't know what would happen. He couldn't blame Angie for tagging along. What she saw as a child was the stuff of nightmares, and, with Larry's help, she'd been able to rationalize it as such, and discard those memories with all the other dreams that can haunt a child's sleep. He also knew Angie was lonely. Sure, she'd never say that to him, and she put on a good front, but Larry knew when his daughter was unhappy. Angie had a fierce loyalty to her father, being there for him when her mother flaked out. Though it filled him with joy to have such a thoughtful, loving daughter, he also felt guilty. Her dedication to him was holding her back. That evening with Paula restored a light and excitement in her Larry hadn't seen in a very long time. It was how Larry wanted to see her all the time, and he feared that would never be the case as long as she stayed at home with him. No, he couldn't be mad. The girls were good for each other. They just got caught up in something bad.

The rain tapered off, and Larry walked out into the yard. Sprinkles dotted his clothes and stuck to his beard, but he didn't mind. His eyes were on the trees. Before he could lose his nerve, he pushed himself forward and walked briskly across the lawn. A nearby squirrel saw his approach and darted away into the shadows. He stopped at the trail's edge and peered inside. Nothing appeared out of sorts and the only sounds were the raindrops pattering and the leaves rustling in the breeze.

Larry cleared his throat, then looked back at the house to confirm he was alone. Satisfied that no one was watching or within earshot, he turned back to the trees.

"Is anyone there?"

The forest did not answer. He looked around nervously, aware how crazy he appeared.

"If you're out there, I'd like you to leave my family alone. We've got no quarrel with you. Whatever happened between you and my brother is done. He's dead. We have no part in that."

Nothing stirred in the forest.

Larry stood for a long time, waiting for any response, but the trees were quiet. The rain picked up again, and Larry felt foolish. Here he was, a grown man, talking to the trees, getting soaked. He shook his head, and made his way back to the house. Maybe things were going to be okay. The girls definitely stirred it up, but maybe it wasn't as serious as he feared. God, he hoped so. Maybe they'd experienced what they call a "residual" haunt. Something like a video on loop, completely unaware of the present. In truth, he hadn't actually seen anything at all. He certainly felt a tension and energy in the air, but perhaps that was fueled by his own fear.

Maybe you got yourself all worked up for nothing.

Relief washed over him and for the first time since that night, he let himself relax. Reaching the porch, he kicked off his boots and stepped inside.

Immediately, he was assaulted by the smell of smoke. He moved quickly to the stove. His first thought was he'd forgotten to turn off the oven when he fried his bacon and eggs for breakfast, but the stove top was cold to the touch.

Electrical? No, it didn't smell like that. It smelled like wood. He sniffed the air and walked into the living room. Stronger, but there was no smoke visible. He followed the aroma down the hallway and into his bedroom.

A large wooden chest sat at the foot of his bed. It was a family heirloom with decorative wicker patterns wrapping across the rounded top. Smoke creeped from the seams. Larry sprang forward and threw open the lid. Smoke billowed out and the sudden influx of oxygen caused the smoldering fire to erupt. Larry stared into the chest, eyes wide in horror. A bundle of sticks lay in the center on top of now blackened and smoldering photo albums, tied together with white ribbon with red polka dots. Flames wiggled and snaked between the branches, spreading through the contents. The chest's inner walls glowed orange like a furnace.

Larry bellowed, then ran back to the kitchen. He threw open the cabinet doors under the sink and pulled a small fire extinguisher from within. The thing had been down there for years and he had no idea if it would even work. He ran back through the house, struggling to pull the pin from the unit. It broke free as he entered the bedroom, and he pointed the nozzle at the chest.

The chest was closed and the smoke was gone. With a defeated groan, he dropped the extinguisher to the floor, and threw open the chest. His eyes bulged and his blood ran cold. The chest's contents were unharmed, but instead of the bundle of burning sticks, the polka dot ribbon now fastened a sheet of paper, rolled loosely into a cylinder. With a quivering hand, he lifted it. His heartbeat pounded in his ears as his fingers gripped the soft fabric. He recognized the ribbon immediately, but now that the urgency of the fire was gone, the meaning hit home. It was Angie's favorite ribbon, a staple of her youth. Very rarely did you ever see Angie without the polka dot ribbon tied up in her hair. Larry blew out a steadying breath and removed the paper. It was dry and stiff, crackling as he unrolled it. He let out a mournful groan and clamped a hand over his mouth.

It was a child's drawing, done in crayon, of a forest. In the trees stood a black figure with yellow eyes.

He'd seen it before. many years ago, when a small girl had nightmares about monsters in the forest and drew a picture so her father could see what she saw.

He'd burnt it in the fireplace himself.

On instinct, he turned his head and looked out the bedroom window overlooking the yard. A figure stood at the trail opening, where he stood only moments before. It blended in with the trees, shifting in and out of view, but it was there. The forest had heard his request.

He had his answer.

CHAPTER 12

Angie sat at the small section of the office counter that served as her desk, transcribing notes from patient exams into their files. It was a busy morning, but the constant activity kept her focused. Idle moments let her mind wander and too often she found herself back in the forest. She'd latched firmly to the belief that everything had been their drunken imaginations. Staying busy allowed her to rationalize. She wasn't a little girl anymore.

Her father had been acting strange since that night. Angie thought he might be mad at her for going out there, but he would let it go in time. She never knew her father to hold a grudge, except maybe against her mom, and on that front she was in total agreement.

"Hey Ang, can you take Mr. Leshner back to room four, please?"

Angie glanced up from her station, and tried to hide a grimace. She'd been so wrapped up transcribing notes that she hadn't paid attention to the people signing in up front. Mr. Leshner was a pervy old man with enough medical problems to keep him coming to the office on a weekly basis.

"Sure thing, Mary," Angie replied in a weak attempt at cheer. She stood. "Mr. Leshner, you can come on back."

The old man looked up and sneered at her, making no effort to hide his eyes crawling up and down her body. "Hello, Angie," the old man said as he shuffled across the room. He reached out a liver-spotted hand for her to shake. "You look lovely this afternoon."

Angie gritted her teeth and took the old man's hand in hers. "Very kind of you to say," she said. He immediately began to rub a finger across her wrist and she snatched her hand back.

Mr. Leshner chuckled and followed her to the hallway leading to the exam rooms. Angie walked quickly, knowing full well that he was staring at her ass. She reached room four and quickly turned to motion him inside.

"You'll have to forgive me," he said, "I'm not as quick as I used to be." He reached the doorway, huffing from exertion. He stopped before entering and leaned toward her. "I can still do some things I used to do just fine, though."

Angie bit down on her lip and refused to acknowledge him. He chuckled again and shuffled into the room. Angie waited while he gingerly climbed onto the step stool and sat down on the crinkly paper rolled out on the exam table.

"What brings you in to see us today, Mr. Leshner?"

"Could you close the door, dear? There's a breeze blowing through, chilling me right to the bone."

Angie hissed through her nose. She'd purposely left the door open to avoid being completely alone with the old creep. "Of course," she said, pushing the door closed.

"I've been having pain in my legs. I got the arthritis, ya know, but this is new."

"Is it a sharp pain or more of an ache?" Angie asked while she wrote down notes for the doctor.

"Mostly an ache, but sometimes I get a sharp pain."

"Have you been keeping up with your medication?"

"Oh yes," Mr. Leshner said.

"Okay. Let me get your vitals." She strapped a blood pressure cuff to his thin arm, slipped the stethoscope underneath, then pumped.

Mr. Leshner grimaced as the cuff tightened on his arm. "That sure is tight. Bet that's not the only thing you got that's tight," he said, then winked.

Angie's mouth dropped open in surprise. Mr. Leshner was always moderately creepy, but he'd never said something *that* vulgar.

"Mr. Leshner, that is entirely inappropriate, and I'll ask you not to talk to me like that."

"Oooh," he said, "I got you riled up, did I?"

"If you don't stop, I'll have to go get Dr. Hendrix and issue a complaint."

Suddenly the mock innocence fell from the old man's face. His eye brows flattened and he licked his lips. "How about you stop running your mouth and put it to better use?" He reached down and squeezed himself through his trousers.

Angie dropped the stethoscope and backed away from the exam table.

"You gonna run away? Just like you always do? Run away like the scared little girl you are. A scared little girl running through the forest. We never forgot you. Oh no, we never forget. When you came back with your little friend, we remembered you. We want you back."

Angie shuffled toward the door, not daring to take her eyes away from the man.

"You can't run forever. We'll take you into the fire. We'll have you then, whether you like it or not. Oh yes, my dear. We will take you... ruin you...eat you."

Angie screamed, threw open the door and ran into the hallway. Dr. Hendrix and Mary stared at her from the counter.

"Ang, what's the matter?" Dr. Hendrix asked with concern.

"Mr. Leshner, he...he..."

Dr. Hendrix pushed past her and entered the exam room.

"Oh lord, Mary, call an ambulance," he shouted.

Angie didn't understand. She inched back toward the exam room and peeked inside.

Mr. Leshner lay on the floor twitching. Thick foam coated his lips and blood dripped from his ears. The stench of human feces filled the air and it was clear he'd soiled himself.

"What happened, Angie, did he fall?" Dr. Hendrix knelt down beside Mr. Leshner.

Angie couldn't speak, only staring as Dr. Hendrix tried to help the man. Mary appeared beside her in the doorway and gasped.

"Oh heavens," she said. "The ambulance is on their way. Angie, what happened?"

Angie only shook her head.

"I think she's in shock," Dr. Hendrix said. "Mary, take her to my office and have her sit for a while?"

Mary took Angie by the shoulders and led her back down the hall to Dr. Hendrix's office behind the reception counter. She directed her to sit, then went back to help the doctor.

Angie rocked back and forth in the chair, wide eyes staring at the wall.

We'll take you in the fire.

CHAPTER 13

"Paula, we worked with you to get a couple days off for the funeral. I understand you lost your aunt, I really do. But you have to understand that I've got a business to run, and I need my employees to be here."

"I know," Paula said, "and I appreciate you working with me. I came down with a bug while I was away."

Her boss sighed into the phone. "Alright, just know these days are counting against you. If your attendance gets to a certain point, then we're going to have to have a hard conversation."

"I understand, and I think I'll be okay to come back tomorrow."

"I hope so."

"Thank you, Mr. Doyle."

"Uh huh," he replied, then hung up the phone.

Paula drooped and hung the phone back on the cradle. *I've got to get it together.*

She wasn't sick, at least not in a traditional sense. She arrived home an hour after her detour along the river bank and hadn't left her apartment since. The doors and windows were locked up tight, and she developed a routine patrol looking out each window for anyone or *anything* unusual. Every sound from the streets below gave her a violent start.

None of the things that happened fit her view of the world. As far as she was concerned, life was difficult and often unfair, but she'd never believed in anything supernatural or evil.

Until now.

There was no explanation for what happened at the river. The things she saw in the forest could be rationalized by alcohol and the power of suggestion. But she wasn't drunk when that man spoke to her. He spoke of things he couldn't know. What did he mean when he said her mother was *in the fire?* She wasn't a spiritual person either, but she liked to think there was something after we die. The thought of her mother trapped by whatever was in those woods tormented her.

Several times, she'd almost called Angie to tell her what happened. The thing holding her back was the other potential reason for all this.

What if she was really losing her mind?

What if she told Angie, and maybe even Larry, about what she saw and they told her to go see a doctor? If they doubted her—questioned her sanity—it would hurt. She wasn't ready to face that.

With no clear direction to follow, she felt frozen in place. She needed time to pass with no more strange occurrences to regain control. She couldn't take a chance on losing her job, and based on the discussion with her boss, it looked like she would have to return to work the next day and face the world. It overwhelmed her, but she had to move on. She made a round, checking locks and windows, then curled up on the couch. After a while, she slept.

A rhythmic tapping noise roused her awake. She blinked sleep from her eyes and squinted at the clock. It was half past nine and darkness had fallen. The yellow glow of street lights outside filtered through the windows. Paula rubbed her face with her palms. She stared into the gloomy shadows of the living room, trying to find her bearings. She only intended to take a nap but hours had passed.

Tap...tap...tap.

The noise finally registered. Her trembling hand twisted the lamp switch. Light bathed the room. Nothing appeared to be out of place. Biting back panic, she stood and walked to the hallway.

Tap...tap...tap.

As she crept, a new sound joined the tapping. A soft, steady hiss. This was a sound she recognized, and it stopped her where she stood.

The shower is running.

Paula wanted to scream. Someone was in her apartment. She knew beyond the shadow of a doubt every door and window was locked, but it didn't matter. They'd gotten in, and turned on the shower. Logic told her to run, Get out of the apartment, run to a neighbor's house and call the police. She could tell from the muted sound of the shower that the bathroom door was closed. If she was quiet, she could get out unnoticed. But, curiosity overruled her instincts and she moved further down the hall, as if on auto-pilot, and peered around the corner.

The bathroom door was indeed closed and the light was on. She could see the glow underneath the door.

Tap..tap...tap.

Whatever the tapping noise was, it was also coming from the bathroom. Slowly, she crept back down the hallway to the kitchen. A knife block sat on the counter, and she pulled the large butcher knife from its slot. She was determined to open the bathroom door, despite the lunacy of not running, but she was not foolish enough to go in unarmed.

Knife in hand, she returned to the hallway and rounded the corner. The closed bathroom door stood six feet away, and she took a steadying breath.

Tap...tap...tap.

Before she could lose her nerve, she twisted the knob and threw the door open. Steam flooded out into the hall, forcing her to back away. The tapping ceased and was replaced by panicked squawking and flapping. Paula stared in wonder at a large sparrow flapping wildly around the bathroom. It flew across the room and bounced off the smoked glass window, then circled around and dove at the window again.

Other than the trapped bird, the bathroom was empty. Paula could see the shower from the doorway and the curtain was pulled wide. The floor around the tub was damp from the water splashing over the side.

Paula dropped the knife and ran to the window. She snapped the lock and pushed it open, then ducked and ran the few feet back to the door, hands over her head. She turned in time to see the bird crash back into the window, this time finding it open and squeezing out into the night.

She stood motionless, trying to make sense of what was happening. A small section of the wall next to the windowsill was punctured and shredded with insulation poking out of the holes. *The tapping,* she thought. The bird was pecking the wall, trying to get out.

But how did it get in?

In a daze, Paula crossed the room to the shower, careful not to slip on the wet floor, and turned off the faucet. She watched the last remnants of water swirl down the drain, then closed the curtain. Nothing made any sense. None of this could be happening, but it was. The thing that gave her pause was this series of events felt *different.* She'd felt danger in the woods and on the river bank. She didn't feel that, now. The air was lighter, and rather than dread, she felt calm.

Paula turned back to close the window, and her eyes fell on the bathroom mirror. She hadn't noticed it before because of the steam, but with the bathroom door and window open, the air cleared.

A message was drawn in the condensation on the mirror. Paula read it over and over until tears blurred her vision and wiped it away. It wasn't the message itself that brought on the tears, but rather the handwriting. She knew it well. She had dozens of birthday and Christmas cards tucked away in a drawer featuring the same neat script —Candy's handwriting.

You have to go back

CHAPTER 14

Larry sat in the kitchen waiting for Angie to wake up. He was afraid of what she might say when he asked the questions he needed to ask, but it couldn't be avoided. He knew something was wrong as soon as Mary called him from the office.

Shock. That's what Dr. Hendrix told Larry. Angie was curled up in a chair, clutching her knees against her chest. She didn't say a word then or the whole way home. The doctor told her to take a few days off to rest up. He offered to prescribe her something to help, but Larry told him that wouldn't be necessary, and he would call if things didn't improve.

Angie went straight to the shower and then to her room. Larry gave her some time, then checked in to find her sound asleep. Since then, he'd been drinking coffee and waiting. He had questions, but he knew one thing for sure. Angie was not in shock because an old man keeled over in the office. She was a nurse, for Christ's sake. She worked with the sick and the dying on a daily basis. No, he knew his daughter, and she was much tougher than that. Something else happened. He thought about his afternoon—the fire, the ribbon, the drawing. The drawing was still there, as far as he knew. He'd dropped it back inside and slammed the lid closed, unable to muster the courage to open it again.

He knew in his gut something similar happened to Angie. His heart broke to know she was being subjected to horrors like this. He couldn't allow it to go on, and he had no intention of stalling any longer with false hope that it would just go away.

Larry finished off what must've been his fourth or fifth cup of coffee, and was getting ready to go wake her up when he heard the door creak and her footsteps padding down the hall. She stepped into the kitchen and looked at him with wide, wet eyes.

"Dad?"

"Yeah?"

"Do you think I'm crazy?"

Larry swallowed the lump in his throat and shook his head. "Today, the chest in my bedroom caught fire. There was a bundle of burning branches inside tied together with white ribbon with red polka dots. The same kind you used to tie up your hair with. I ran to the kitchen to get the extinguisher, and when I got back it was gone. Instead, there was a picture you drew of the monsters in the woods when you were a little girl. A picture I burnt in the fireplace to keep you from thinking about it. Do you think I'm crazy?"

Angie's face went pale and she put a hand over her mouth.

"What happened to you at the office? I need to know."

"Something happened to Mr. Leshner."

"He died in the office, I know that."

"No," Angie said. "Well, yes, he died, but that's not what I mean. He's always a creep, but he said terrible things to me." She blushed and looked away. "Things I won't say to you. But, then he said things about the woods. He said they would take me into the fire."

Larry winced.

"Dad, what's happening?"

"I'm going to tell you, but I think we should call Paula. I'm afraid these things may be happening to her, too."

"Is it because we went to the cemetery?"

"It must be. I thought it was over, but it looks like it's not."

"You thought *what* was over? What aren't you telling me?"

"It's a long story, and one I don't want to tell twice, so we need to know if Paula is affected or not."

"Paula's back in Ohio. This can't be happening to her back home, can it?"

"I don't know, but I think we should find out."

"How? Do we call her and say, hey Paula, has any weird shit been happening to you since you left?"

"No," Larry answered. "We'll call her and ask how she's holding up. If anything's going on with her, I'll be able to tell."

Angie shook her head. "This is crazy. What are we even talking about?"

"I promise I'll tell you everything. I need to know if Paula's okay, first."

"Okay, let's call her. I don't care if it's late. If you won't tell me what's going on until we talk to her, then I'm not waiting until tomorrow." Angie stomped across the kitchen to the counter and the phone receiver. Before she could reach for it, the red light pulsed and the phone rang. Angie turned and locked eyes with Larry. He nodded. Angie picked up the phone and handed it to Larry.

"Hello?"

"Larry, it's Paula."

"Hey, Paula," Larry said, trying to keep his voice calm and level. "Is everything alright?"

"That's why I'm calling. Something happened on my way home the other day, and something just happened in my apartment. This is going to sound crazy, but I think I need to come back down there."

Larry closed his eyes and dropped his head.

"I think I'd rather talk about it in person. I don't know if you'll believe it on the phone."

"Oh, I think I might," Larry said. "We've got some things to tell you about as well. When can you come?"

"I'll leave first thing in the morning."

"We'll be here. You be careful. And Paula, I'm sorry this is happening."

"Do you know what it is?"

"Not entirely, but I know enough to be afraid."

"It's our fault, isn't it? We did something when we went to the cemetery?"

"It doesn't matter, now. What matters is what we do about it. I'll tell you and Angie both everything I know when you get here, tomorrow. Until then, take care of yourself."

Larry ended the call and dropped the phone on the table.

"Dad, are we gonna be okay?"

Larry stared back at her. "I sure hope so."

CHAPTER 15

Much to Paula's surprise, the drive back to Larry's house was uneventful. She'd barely slept the night before, waiting for the next shoe to drop, but all was quiet.

She packed a small bag before she went to bed, then rose early. Her boss wouldn't be in the office until seven, but she called anyway and left a message. Unforeseen circumstances caused her to leave town, and she would be contacting HR to discuss a leave of absence. Paula hoped mentioning HR would scare him off and buy her time to deal with whatever this was.

Unforeseen circumstances. That was one way to put it. One thing she knew for sure, Larry had answers. She couldn't fathom what it could be, but she believed him when he said he would tell her and Angie everything. Paula found comfort in knowing Angie was in the dark as well. It made her feel less like a bystander.

She made good time, stopping only once for gas, and pulled into Larry's driveway shortly after noon. Both Larry and Angie were seated on the back porch. Larry stood and waved. Paula climbed out of the car and walked to the porch.

"Welcome back, I guess," Larry said.

"I wanted my next visit to be under happier circumstances."

"I wanted the same."

"Hey, Ang," Paula said, waving across the porch. "You got any more lightning lemonade? I think we might need some."

Angie smiled weakly. "Not today."

Paula nodded and eyed Angie with concern. She looked pale and exhausted, nothing like the vibrant young woman from a few days before. "You okay?"

"Are you?"

Paula shook her head. "Not even a little bit."

Larry motioned to an empty fold-out chair beside Angie. "Go ahead and sit down. We've got a lot to talk about."

Paula crossed the porch and sat down. She reached over and squeezed Angie's hand, and was relieved when Angie squeezed back.

Larry sat down in a large wooden rocking chair that creaked under his weight. "Where do we even start?"

"Well, let me tell you what happened to me after I left here. You said some strange things have happened here since I've been gone, but *strange* is a broad word. What happened to me is not strange. It's impossible."

Larry and Angie exchanged knowing glances, then Larry nodded. "Go ahead."

Paula told them about her stop at the river and the homeless man who approached her. They listened in silence while she quoted his words from memory. Then, she told them about the snake in the water that was actually a tongue. "It was the same face Angie and I saw in the woods," Paula said, turning to Angie.

Angie stared back in horror, and Paula knew right away she believed her.

"That man, he said King's Creek Cemetery, said it more than once. He *knew* where I had been. He said my mother was there."

"You're mom isn't buried there, is she?" Angie asked.

"No," Larry answered, "she's not."

"I said the same thing, and he said he didn't mean she was buried there."

Larry dropped his head and pinched the bridge of his nose. "So, what did you do?"

"I ran. I ran back to the car and got the hell out of there."

"Okay," Larry said. "I think I speak for us both when I say we believe you. We've had equally strange experiences."

Paula listened in growing distress as Larry told her about the burning chest and Angie's childhood drawing. When he finished, Angie took over and told her about Mr. Leshner at the doctor's office.

"Jesus, Angie, I'm sorry."

"For what?"

"This is all my fault. I don't know what's going on, but it didn't start until we went into the woods, and you never would have gone if I didn't push you."

"We didn't know," Angie said, then turned to Larry. "We *still* don't know. Dad, what is happening?"

Larry started to speak, but Paula cut him off. "One more thing," she said. She told them about the bathroom, the bird, and the message on the mirror.

"My God," Larry said.

"That's why I called. It's why I had to come back. Candy told me too."

"You really think it was her?" Angie asked. "Whatever this is has been fucking with us—"

"Language," Larry said sternly.

Angie rolled her eyes. "Sorry. I'm just saying, are you sure it wasn't this thing trying to trick you into coming back?"

"I don't think so," Paula said. "It wasn't like the forest or the river. I was scared, sure, but the atmosphere was different. It didn't feel menacing. When I was at the river, I felt like I was in danger. I didn't feel that in my apartment. I felt urgency, like there was no time to waste."

"I think you're right about that," Larry said.

"Okay," Angie said. "Enough dancing around the story. You said you would tell us everything when we were together, and here we are. There's monsters in the woods, ghosts in our houses, and omnipresent homeless guys at the river. I think I'm primed for whatever you got next, old man."

Larry stopped rocking and stared at Angie with a dumbfounded look on his face.

In spite of everything, Paula laughed—a small chuckle at first, then it blossomed into a full-bellied guffaw. Angie snickered and then joined in. Larry shook his head in amazement.

"You two beat all I ever seen. You're both like Candy. She always seemed to find the humor in everything." Larry sighed. "Well, maybe not everything. She's part of this story too. And, you're right, Angie. It's time to fill you girls in on what I think we're dealing with."

The girls quieted down.

He took a deep breath then exhaled and looked Paula in the eyes.

"It started when your momma got sick."

CHAPTER 16

"Do you remember back at the funeral when I said sometimes things aren't quite how we remember them to be?"

Paula nodded.

"This is like that. Your momma was sick for a long time, a lot longer than anybody knew. She was a tough woman, though, and she didn't let it keep her down. Being tough is a good thing, but it can also come back to haunt you. That's what happened to Claire. She ignored it and pushed through for so long that by the time she asked for help, it was too late to do anything about it. Maybe it wouldn't have mattered, but maybe it would have. If she'd gone to the doctor sooner, maybe they could have saved her. But, she didn't, and that was that."

Larry paused for a moment while he collected his thoughts. It felt strange to be telling this story now, after all these years, but it was also a relief to unburden his soul.

"What you may not remember," he continued, "is your father, my brother, loved your momma very much. He didn't always act like it, and he did some stupid things, but he was crazy about Claire. When we found out what was wrong with her, and there wasn't nothing they could do to help her, David lost his mind. If the doctors couldn't do anything with traditional medicine, then he decided to pursue—*other* alternatives."

"Other alternatives?" Angie asked. "Like home remedies?"

"I wish that's all it was," Larry said. "These mountains have a rich history, and some folks are not too keen on letting the old ways go. Paula, I know you've seen it yourself. Leaving these hills or coming back can almost feel like time travel."

Paula nodded.

"Some of those old traditions are what most people consider folklore. Fairy tales and make believe. *Magic*. In my experience, and after the last few days I think you two will agree, it's not all superstition." He paused and looked at the girls. Both were stone-faced without a trace of doubt. Satisfied, he continued. "I don't know that I would call it magic, but there is definitely more to this world than science is willing to admit. And ain't all of it good."

"So what did my dad do?" Paula asked.

"He went deeper into the mountains. We're pretty much in the middle of nowhere here, but there are places even more remote in these hills. Folks who like their privacy and have no interest in giving up the old ways. There's an old feller up there, name's Crenshaw, Albert Crenshaw, and it's well known in these parts that he dabbles in stuff you shouldn't be messing with."

"Like black magic? Occult stuff?" Angie asked.

"David knew about him, and he'd lost faith in doctors and prayer. So, he drove out to Crenshaw's place and asked for help. Crenshaw pulled out his books and gave David a spell or ritual to contact the spirits of the mountain. I don't know the details. I don't care to know, either. What I do know is David went out to the woods one night and worked this spell."

"How do you know this?" Paula asked.

"David told me and Candy after we confronted him about how he was acting. At the time, we thought the same as you, that he was out running around, chasing women and avoiding his responsibilities. I didn't believe him, at first. But, the longer things went on, the more clear it was *he* believed what he told us. Even then, I thought it more likely David had gone mad." Larry paused and shook his head, then stared out at the forest. "Now though, I guess I've changed my tune."

"He did it in the cemetery, didn't he?" Angie asked. "The ritual?"

Larry nodded. "He did."

"Since we're having this conversation, I guess it worked?" Paula asked.

"The ritual worked, yes. He summoned *spirits*. Bad ones. As you can guess, he did not get what he wanted. He made a deal with the devil and the devil does what he always does. He lied."

"What was the deal?" Paula asked.

"David offered his soul to save Claire."

"Hold on," Angie interjected, "are we talking about *the Devil* with a capital D?"

"I don't know," Larry said. "It doesn't matter, does it?"

Angie started to reply, then fell silent.

"So this thing promised to save Mother in exchange for his soul, but lied. Then what happened?"

"Well, your mother didn't get better. She died. David was lost. He'd disappear for days in the woods trying to draw out the spirits, leaving you and your brother alone. The spirits tormented him, mocked him, drove him to madness. I know you thought he was off running around with other women, but that wasn't true. Candy and I both knew his story by then, but we couldn't put that burden on you two. It felt awful to let you go on believing he was bar hopping and sleeping around, but the alternative was even worse."

Paula sniffed and wiped her nose. Larry noticed fresh tears on her cheeks, and his heart broke for her. He wanted to stop and console her, but they needed to hear the rest.

"David continued to decline, and things got worse. Your brother's accident happened. I hate to say this, and I don't know it to be absolute truth, but I believe these spirits might have had a hand in that. Another way to torment David."

"Jesus," Angie said, dropping her head into her hands.

Paula sniffed again and shook her head.

"Not long after that, you turned eighteen and left. Your Dad was too far gone to express it to you, but he was relieved. Not because he didn't want you around, but because he was afraid something would happen to you, like it did to Lonny. After you were gone, Candy and I tried our best to help him, but it was too late. The night before he died, he showed up here. We sat right on this porch, and he told me he'd figured it out. Said he knew how to fix it. I couldn't talk any sense into him and he took off. That next day, Candy and I found him dead at his house. Coroner called it a heart attack, and maybe it was, but it wasn't a natural cause. Of that I am sure."

Larry let the silence settle. After years of keeping secrets, he felt hollow having let them loose. When neither girl spoke, he continued.

"We thought it was over. We knew you wouldn't come back for his funeral, and didn't blame you, knowing what you thought of him. I'm sorry to have let you keep believing that, because David truly did love you and your brother both."

Paula nodded and patted Larry on the leg. "I understand."

"But, now it's back," Angie said.

"It looks that way," Larry said. "My guess was with David gone, and Paula far away, this thing went dormant. When you came back and went out there to the cemetery, you woke it up. And also, and this is the part that's tearing me up inside above all else, based on what happened to you, and what that bum by the river told you, I don't think any of their souls are at rest. I think this monster has them trapped, and I think you, Paula, are the missing piece. This thing wants the whole family, and God help me, I don't know what to do."

CHAPTER 17

Paula listened in stunned silence. The story Larry told went against the grain of everything she thought she knew about her father and the world, but she believed every word. The impact of that epiphany was catastrophic. Years of misplaced hate, anger, and resentment toward her father swelled into a wave of torment. Seeking help from black magic was a poor decision, but he did it out of a love she didn't know he was capable of.

"Jesus, Dad," Angie said. "Things have been happening to all of us, so I don't know if it's fair to say this thing, this *evil*, is just after Paula."

"Maybe not," Larry said, "but my gut says that's what it wants. I think it came after us as a means to help get Paula to come back. And, it worked."

"No, I was coming back anyway," Paula said. She turned to Larry. "I think you're right. It took my parents and my brother, and now it wants me."

Angie moaned in defeat. "What are we going to do?"

"*We* aren't going to do anything. This thing is after me, and I won't drag you two into the line of fire."

"Bullshit!" Angie snapped.

"No, you won't do this alone," Larry said. "I won't stand for that. We'll do this together."

"I can't let you two get hurt. I've been alone for a long time, and you two have reminded me what it's like to belong. I won't let you put yourselves at risk."

"We're already at risk," Angie said. "Besides, we have no idea what to do."

"Oh, I have a plan," Paula said.

"You do?" Larry asked.

"This guy in the mountains, Crenshaw, I'm going to find him and find out what I have to do to end this."

Larry shook his head vehemently. "That's a bad idea, Paula. I told you what happened to your father when he went down that path. It's a mistake to follow in his footsteps. That road only goes one way."

"This is different. We're not trying to save someone, we're trying to cast these demons or whatever the hell they are out of our lives."

"I don't like it," Angie said.

"Whatever is out there, it's unnatural, so it's going to take unnatural means to fight back." Paula stared out at the woods. "I'm done letting it come after us. I'm ready to go after *it*."

"Can I make a suggestion, before we jump straight to seeking out the black magic hermit in the mountains?" Larry asked.

"Please," Angie said.

"We don't know exactly what this thing is. We've used a lot of words—monsters, creatures, demons. One thing I think we all agree on is *evil*. This thing is evil. I believe in the good book. There's light and dark in this world. There's power in light to fight the darkness. You said it yourself, Paula. We need to cast this evil out. In my eyes, only God can do that."

Paula shook her head. "I don't believe a few prayers are going to save the day here, Uncle Larry."

Angie frowned. "Dad, I don't know. Are you saying we go to a church and ask for help casting demons out of the forest before they kill us? They'll lock us up in a psych ward."

"Not exactly," Larry said. "We do have an inside track with the church, ya know?"

Angie looked at Larry quizzically, then her eyes widened. "You mean Grover?"

"Who?" Paula asked.

"Dad's cousin, Grover. Remember? Old cartwheel at Candy's funeral?"

"Oh," Paula said, connecting the name with the face. "Yeah, I don't think he'll be able to help us."

"We don't know that," Larry said.

Paula sighed. "Do you think it's a good idea to bring another person into this? As far as we know, this is contained to us. I don't like the idea of exposing someone else."

"I agree with you there. I don't like it either, but I think we need to try. Maybe we don't have to tell him everything."

"Dad, prayers aren't going to help us. If Grover can actually help, he'll need to know what we're up against."

"I still think it's worth a shot. Grover is more capable than you're giving him credit for. And, like I said, I believe there's power there." Larry stood and stepped to the back door. "I'll go give him a call and see if he can meet with us. No details yet, just that we want advice from him. We can figure out the rest when we get there."

Paula watched him go inside then turned to Angie. "I don't think this will work."

"Me neither, but I hate your plan to go learn black magic in the mountains to fight demons."

The girls stared at each other and burst into another fit of laughter.

"It's so not funny, but if I don't laugh I'll cry or lose my mind," Paula said between chuckles.

"I hear ya," Angie said. "I really hope we can end this and have a *normal* relationship. I'd love to hang out without scary shit happening."

"Me too," Paula said.

The screen door creaked open, and Larry stepped through. "He's home and happy to host us."

"I doubt he'll still be happy after we tell him what's going on," Angie said.

"How far away is he?" Paula asked.

"About thirty minutes. Not too far."

"Let's go. I'm done waiting for things to happen."

Larry nodded and led the way to the driveway.

"I'll drive," Angie said.

Paula climbed into the back seat and stared at the forest as they pulled away. Nothing moved in the trees, but she knew they were being watched. She thought of her family, cursed by whatever evil lurked in the shadows. Revenge boiled in her stomach. *I'm coming for you.*

CHAPTER 18

Grover Hollis hung up the phone and smiled. He was pleasantly surprised to hear from his cousin Larry. They'd been fairly close as children, as tends to be the case with big families, but went separate ways as adults.

Grover embraced the church with all his heart. Everything in his life was meant to serve the Lord. Larry was a good Christian man, but he didn't have the same passion. Grover knew some people viewed their faith as a class status, peering down their noses at the non-believers. He didn't know what they were doing at services on Sunday, but it wasn't listening to the message of Jesus Christ. Grover had love for everyone, and relished any chance he got to provide counsel.

Counsel is what Larry was after. He said he wanted to stop by along with his daughter Angie and niece Paula. Grover was overjoyed for the visit. He hadn't gotten a chance to speak with Paula much at Candace's funeral, and he was delighted to get to see her again. Larry hadn't given any specifics as to why they wanted to visit, only that they could use his advice on things of a *spiritual* nature.

This pleased Grover even more. Getting to visit with family was a treat in its own regard, but a visit with family focused on spreading the gospel was what he lived for. Feeling full of spirit, he rose from his recliner and shuffled to the kitchen to brew some coffee and tea for his guests. A pastry tray might be in order, as well. He put a pot of water on to boil and turned toward the pantry. Halfway across the kitchen, he paused. The crucifix on the wall by the window was knocked off center, with the crucified Jesus tilted at a forty-five degree angle.

Strange, Grover thought. He stepped toward the window and straightened the cross, then admired it for a moment. It was large, silver, with delicate attention to detail. He kept crucifixes in every room, but this was his favorite. He studied the new alignment, decided it was still slightly off center, and reached for it again. Before his fingers touched the cold metal, the cross shifted and spun, then stopped again, upside down.

Grover flinched. *Good Heavens, that's a terrible omen.* He grabbed the cross and corrected it again, making extra sure it was securely fastened on the wall. He shivered, unsettled by the peculiar activity. He whispered a short prayer, then turned back to the pantry. As he scooted jars and cans around, searching for his serving platter, a heavy thump echoed from somewhere in the house. Grover paused.

"That you, Whiskers?" he called out. *That old cat better not be climbing on shelves again.* Whiskers was a very old and very overweight tabby, but he still had enough spunk in him to be mischievous when he took a notion. Grover returned to the living room, expecting to find the old cat prancing around with whatever prize he'd knocked loose. Instead, Whisker's lay curled up in his bed next to the recliner, snoring softly.

"Whiskers?"

The cat's nose twitched, but his eyes remained closed.

Grover turned his eyes to the rest of the room. Nothing was out of place. But through the open door at the end of the hall he could make out a book on the floor. With a shiver, he stepped timidly through the living room and into the hall.

You're being foolish, he thought. *A book fell off a shelf is all. It's not like there's an intruder waiting to whack me over the head when I step through the door.*

Still, irrational fear gripped him. As his study came into view, he recognized the displaced book—a large leatherbound family Bible. He'd inherited it from his mother, and it was filled with notes, highlighted scriptures, loose documents, and photographs. Papers and photos were scattered around the book, dumped loose from the impact. Grover scanned the room. He was alone, but he didn't *feel* alone. He turned to the bookshelf and noted the wide opening where the Bible had sat. Dust streaked the front ledge of the shelf where the book was dragged out of place.

"What in the world?"

He knelt and scooped up the items around the Bible, stacking them neatly. A piece of paper lying face down caught his eye. All the documents he kept in this book were old—cracked, yellowing papers and faded photographs. This paper was crisp and white, as if it had only just come off a press. His brow furrowed and he flipped the page.

It was a coroner's report of an autopsy. Grover's heart pounded, large swelling beats thudding in his ears. His face burned red and his breathing came in quick puffs.

What is this?

The name at the top was Grover Michael Hollis. He read it over and over again, not believing his own eyes. Beads of sweat appeared on his face. Suddenly the room felt very warm. He scanned the page further. The autopsy date was three days from now.

Cause of Death: Heart Attack.

Dear Jesus.

The report fell from his trembling fingers. His eyes landed on a photograph on the floor where the report was before. It must have been underneath the paper and he hadn't noticed. He snatched it up and flipped it over.

In the photo, he saw himself kneeling in his study, staring at a photo. The family Bible lay open on the floor. A figure stood in the doorway behind him. Its body was draped in shadow, but the face was clearly visible. Bright yellow eyes peered down, above a hideous smile filled with jagged, razor-like teeth.

Grover choked out a sob. A hand pressed gently onto his shoulder, and in his peripheral, long dirty fingers with torn nails dug into his shirt.

"God help me," Grover whispered.

CHAPTER 19

"That's it, right there," Larry said, pointing at a small brick house.

Angie nodded and steered the car into the driveway. The yard sloped uphill toward the house, but the drive wrapped around to the side. She'd been here before, but not since childhood. She turned off the car, and they piled out.

Grover lived on a mostly-empty stretch of county road. There were other houses, but none were visible from Grover's place. The house was well kept—the grass meticulously mowed with a grid pattern, the flower bed flourished, framed with dark brown mulch and not a single weed. A decorative sign leaned against the wall on the front porch. KEEP JESUS IN YOUR HEART AND YOU'LL ALWAYS BE HOME.

Larry scanned the house and the yard. "I figured he'd be on us before we could even get out of the car."

"Let's get this over with," Paula said.

Angie nodded and they followed Larry onto the porch. He pulled open the screen and knocked twice.

"What's that sound?" Paula asked.

Larry turned his head, listening. "I'm not sure."

Angie noticed the front window was cracked open, and she leaned toward it. A steady, high-pitched whistle sounded inside. "Teapot, maybe?"

"Probably," Larry replied. "Grover never misses a chance to entertain. Bet he didn't hear me knock." He twisted the door knob, found it unlocked, and pushed it open. "Hey, Grover?"

An orange flash burst through the open door, followed by a screeching howl, sending Angie backwards with a squeal. They turned and watched a large cat shoot off the porch and away from the house.

"Ah, hell," Larry said. "Grover! Whiskers ran right out of the house on me." He turned to the girls and lowered his voice. "He's had that cat for fifteen years or better, and I've never seen the lazy thing so much as trot. Come on."

Angie and Paula locked eyes. Something wasn't right. Angie could feel it, and Paula did too. Nervously, Angie followed Larry into the house with Paula trailing behind.

The living room was empty, and the teapot continued its shrill report. Larry led them into the kitchen. "Grover, I think it's ready."

He stopped in the doorway when he found the kitchen empty. His posture stiffened.

"I don't like this, Dad."

"Me either," Larry replied. He stepped quickly to the stove and removed the pot from the burner. The whistling faded and the house fell into eerie silence. "Didn't look like he was outside anywhere."

Angie leaned back into the living room and looked down the hall. Only one doorway was visible from her position, but it was closed.

"Grover!" Larry shouted, then pushed past the girls back the way they'd come. He stomped through the living room and down the hall. "Grover!" His shouts were rising in pitch.

The girls followed him down the hall. Larry peeked his head in each room then moved to the next. His boots echoed loudly in the narrow hall. Angie's stomach churned, and she stared at the closed door ahead.

He's in there, she thought. *He's in there, and he's not okay.*

"Come on, Grover," Larry shouted again.

He threw open the closed door and moaned.

Angie didn't want to look. She collapsed against the wall and closed her eyes. Paula walked past and mumbled something to Larry.

"Angie, go call an ambulance. Hurry!"

She opened her eyes and met her father's gaze. If they needed an ambulance, maybe he was still alive.

"Go!"

She nodded, then ran back through the house. A phone rested on the table next to the recliner by the front window, and she snatched up the receiver and pounded the numbers.

"9-1-1, what's your emergency?"

"We need an ambulance."

"Who needs an ambulance, ma'am?"

"Grover, my cousin, my dad's cousin. Grover."

"Okay, and what is wrong with Grover?"

Angie paused. She didn't know what to say. Her mind shuffled through options and settled.

"Maybe a heart attack, we're not sure."

"What's the address?"

Shit.

"Dad," Angie called, "what's the address here?"

"822 Baron Avenue," Larry shouted back.

"822 B—" Angie's voice froze in her throat. Outside, a figure climbed through the trees across the road from the house. It crawled on all fours, moving smoothly from branch to branch among the treetops. Birds burst into flight as the thing neared them.

"Ma'am? What's the address?"

Angie couldn't move. The figure stopped moving, then dropped backwards so it hung upside down, facing the house. Branches and leaves kept it mostly covered, but a stiff wind was blowing through and as the leaves swayed she caught glimpses of the face.

"Ma'am? Are you still there?"

Suddenly, the phone jerked out of her hand, breaking her trance.

"It's 822 Baron Avenue. Please, hurry," Paula said, then hung up the phone. "What is it, Ang?"

Angie let out a muffled sob, then tipped her head toward the window. Paula looked outside, then grabbed her and pulled her away from the window.

"Don't look at it," Paula whispered. She wrapped her arms around Angie and hugged her tight. "Don't look."

Angie buried her face in Paula's shoulder. Larry stepped into the living room.

"What happened?"

"It's out there," Paula said, "in the trees. Don't look at it. It wants us to know it did this."

"Goddammit!" Larry screamed. He stomped across the room and threw open the door.

"Dad, no!"

Larry paid her no mind and rushed out onto the porch. The girls scrambled after him and huddled in the doorway. Larry stood still, his posture rigid, glaring at the figure in the trees. Its yellow eyes flashed as the leaves brushed across its face. For a tense moment, no one moved or spoke. The staredown was broken when the soft wail of a siren became audible in the distance. The figure smiled, lashed out its tongue, then scrambled deeper into the trees, moving with animal-like agility, and vanished from sight.

Angie walked up behind Larry and put her hand on his shoulder.

"Dad?"

"I'm going to kill that thing," Larry said.

He turned toward her, and Angie flinched at the intensity in his eyes.

"If it's the last thing I ever do in this life, I will kill that God forsaken thing."

CHAPTER 20

Paula held the screen door open for the paramedics while they pushed the stretcher outside. Grover lay still, a white sheet pulled up over his head. Larry and Angie stood in the driveway talking to the coroner. Paula could hear bits of the conversation. *Likely a heart attack. They can come out of nowhere. Happens all the time. Blocked arteries can go undetected until the big one hits.*

The cause of death might very well be a heart attack, but it was not a natural cause, that was for sure. Larry nodded in agreement, mouth tight, not giving any indication of foul play.

Grover was loaded into the ambulance, and the paramedics pulled away. The coroner shook Larry's hand and returned to his vehicle.

"I'm sorry for your loss," he said. "Larry, I'll be in touch in the next day or two."

"Thank you," Larry replied. His voice was void of emotion.

The coroner backed out of the driveway, leaving the three of them alone. Larry walked back to the porch, locked the front door and pulled it closed. He turned and found the girls staring at him.

"What do we do now?" Angie asked.

"We do what Paula said we should do."

"Crenshaw," Paula said.

"Yup. I don't like it now any more than I did before, but my decision cost Grover his life. No one else is going to suffer for this. I still believe God is on our side, and I can't explain why he let this happen to Grover. But, I learned a long time ago there's nothing to gain from questioning God's plan. We only have one path left. Fight fire with fire."

"Do you know where to find this guy?" Angie asked.

"Not exactly, but I know people who do know. Let's get back to the house, and you girls sit tight while I go talk to a few folks and get directions."

"No," Paula said.

"Absolutely not," Angie said. "You're not going anywhere without us. I don't think it's safe for any of us to be alone."

Larry shook his head, but Paula cut him off.

"She's right, Larry. We have to stay together until this is done. We already know there is no limit to this thing's reach. If we separate, it will know, and it will come after us. If it can take us out one by one, it will."

"Fine," Larry said, defeated. "I just wish I could handle this without involving you two, is all."

"I know you do, Dad, and we love you for it, but this isn't yours to carry alone."

"We're stronger together," Paula said.

Larry nodded and pulled both girls into a hug. "I love you both. Let's get moving."

A squeaky *meow* came from behind them, and Angie squealed and spun.

Whiskers stood on the porch, pawing at the screen door, meowing in protest.

"Oh, poor kitty," Angie said. She walked to the door and squatted down, holding out a hand for the cat.

Whiskers studied her for a moment, then stepped cautiously to her. He sniffed at her hand, then licked her finger. He meowed again, then allowed her to pick him up.

Angie groaned as she stood. "Wow, you're heavy. Dad, we can't leave him here."

"I know. We'll drop him off at home and fix him up a bed. It's on the way, anyway."

Angie handed the cat off to Larry, and they loaded up into her car.

Thirty minutes later, Whiskers was curled up on an old blanket in Larry's living room with a bowl of water set out in the kitchen. If he had any anxiety from leaving his home of fifteen years, he showed no sign, and snored softly.

"So where are we going?" Paula asked. She stood near the door, bouncing from one foot to the other, eager to be on the road.

"I've got an old buddy in town. He knows a little bit about everybody around here. He'll know how to get to Crenshaw's place."

"You mean Gary?" Angie asked, disgust on her face.

Larry rolled his eyes. "Yes, Gary."

"Gary's full of shit, dad. He'll get us lost for sure."

"I've got more faith in him than you do, and I'm confident he'll know the way." Larry glanced out the window. "Daylight's burning on us. Let's go."

"Why do you think Gary is full of shit?" Paula asked as they left the house.

"He's an old town gossip, spreading rumors and twisting stories to suit him."

"That is true, but doesn't mean he doesn't know where people live. A fella like Gary that enjoys talking about people is well served to know who people are and where you can find them."

"I guess," Angie said. She dropped into the driver seat and started the car. "You know where to find him, I assume?"

"Yup. Right now, he'll be getting ready to head down to Scooter's."

"Classy," Angie teased.

"If we hurry, we'll catch him before he leaves and save us from having to go in there."

"I'm not going in Scooter's, mountain demons be damned," Angie said.

"Just drive," Larry said.

Paula kept her eyes glued to the passing landscape, waiting for the thing in the trees to come after them, but the journey was blissfully uneventful. As they rolled into town, Paula was struck by deja vu. She'd avoided this area during her visit for the funeral, but the unchanged appearance of the run-down buildings was a wave of nostalgia. This place was a time capsule, untouched by technology's steady march. It was hard to imagine the bustle of city life could even exist in the same world.

Angie steered the car onto a small residential street. Near the end, Larry pointed to a green house with a rusted-out pickup truck in the driveway. A man in jeans and a red flannel shirt with the sleeves rolled up to the elbows stood near the truck, digging in his pockets.

"Hot damn, we're in luck," Larry said. "Pull in behind him."

Angie slowed and parked in the driveway behind the truck. The man swiveled in their direction, swaying slightly with the effort. "Looks like he's done some pre-gaming before going to Scooter's."

Larry rolled down the window and leaned his head out. "Hey, Gary!"

Gary squinted, then beamed a smile at them. "Lare-Bear, is that you?"

Angie snorted. "Lare-Bear? Oh my God, that's amazing."

Paula snickered from the backseat.

Gary stumbled toward the car. "Good to see you, buddy! To what do I owe the pleasure?" He leaned forward with his hands on his knees and peered inside. "Hello there, ladies. Miss Angie, I'd know you anywhere, but I'm afraid I don't know your friend here."

"This is my niece, Paula."

Gary scratched his chin and considered, then his eyes lit up with recognition. "Paula? David's little girl? Well, don't that beat all. You're all grown up. I haven't seen you since you was just a little thing."

"Yeah, I've been gone a long time."

"You sure have."

"Listen, Gary. Since Paula's back, we were thinking of visiting some family. Thing is, I haven't done the best job keeping up with folks. We've got a cousin lives up the mountain, but I can't for the life of me remember how to get there. I know it's out by Crenshaw's place."

"Hmm," Gary said. "I don't know of many folk livin out that way. Most people don't *want* to live close to that old coot."

"I know," Larry said. "But, still, I think if I got out there it would jog my memory. What's the quickest way to get there?"

Gary looked at Larry, then to Paula, then back to Larry. Suspicion clouded his face. "A cousin, ya say?"

"Yeah, a distant cousin. Name's Robert Weaver."

"Robert Weaver. Never heard that name before."

"Yeah, he keeps to himself. Probably why he doesn't mind living up there."

Gary cocked an eyebrow.

He knows, Paula thought.

"Can you help me out, Gary?"

"Just take the county road up the mountain. Two or three miles up there's a gravel road veers off to the left. Follow it and keep going another couple miles. You'll come to a split in the road. Crenshaw's place is up the right a ways."

"That's right," Larry said. "It's coming back to me. Think instead of going right to Crenshaw's, I go left."

"Uh huh," Gary said.

"Been a big help, Gary. I appreciate you."

Gary looked into the car, flashing glances at each passenger, then settling back on Larry. "Steer clear of Crenshaw's place. I don't know what you've gotten yourselves into, but I don't think I believe you're tracking down a cousin I never heard of. Crenshaw ain't never done no good for nobody. Whatever you got in mind, I'd think awful hard about it. You of all people should know that, Larry."

Larry shifted uncomfortably in the seat. "Nah, Gary, don't worry about us. Out visiting is all. I know better than to go foolin' around with the likes of Albert Crenshaw."

"I sure hope so," Gary said.

"I'll see you around, Gary. Take care."

"You do the same."

Angie backed out of the driveway and pointed the car back the way they came. Paula looked out the back window. Gary stood in his driveway watching them go. As they drove away, Paula watched him draw a cross on his chest and shake his head.

I hope your prayers work. We're gonna need all the help we can get.

CHAPTER 21

It was only a little past five when Angie turned onto the dirt path acting as Albert Crenshaw's driveway, but already the sun was dipping low in the sky. A thick canopy of trees lined the path, blocking out what remained of the fading light.

The house was little more than a shack. The front porch sagged and looked like it could collapse at any time. Large sections of the frame were rotted away. A pile of split logs lay on the ground beside the house. A single window showed flickering orange light. A steady stream of gray smoke rose from the chimney.

"Wow," Angie said.

"Certainly lives up to reputation," Paula said. She leaned forward between the two front seats and stared at the house. "Looks like he's home."

"Let me talk to him first. You two stay in the car. I haven't had any dealings with the man in many years. I don't know how he'll take to strangers showing up on his property."

"I definitely wasn't going to be the one to knock," Angie said jokingly, but her face showed no trace of humor.

Angie parked, and Larry stepped out. Cool, moist air blew in through the open car door, and Angie shivered. This deep in the mountain, the temperature dropped at least ten degrees. Larry closed the door, then walked toward the house. Angie rolled down the passenger window and leaned toward it. Paula perched herself behind the passenger seat, eyes glued on Larry.

The ground was thick with fallen leaves and branches, and Larry's footfalls crunched loudly in the clearing. He was ten feet from the treacherously unstable wooden stairs to the porch when a voice called out from inside.

"Who the hell are you?"

Larry froze, then took a cautionary step back.

"It's Larry Tompkins. Do you remember me? My brother was David Tompkins."

"Hmm, David Tompkins?"

"Yes, do you remember?"

"'Course I remember. David was a damn fool. What's done is done with him. Don't mean nothing to me."

"That's why I'm here," Larry said. "I thought it was done, too, but it's not. I've got my daughter, Angie, and David's daughter, Paula, in the car there with me. We've found ourselves in a bit of trouble, and I think you might be the only person who knows how to help us."

"What happened to David was his own damn fault. I don't want no trouble for it."

"Whatever David did didn't work out, we all know that. Trouble is, whatever evil it was he got to foolin' with has come back."

"What's that got to do with me? I didn't conjure nothing."

Larry started to reply, but stopped when he heard a car door open behind him. He turned to see Paula standing outside the car.

"Mr. Crenshaw? My name is Paula Tompkins. David was my father. I didn't know it then, but I know now what my dad was trying to do. He lost everything for it. He lost my mom, he lost Lonny, and then he lost his own life. I've been gone a long time, but since I came back, this thing is after me and my family here. It's not going to stop until it takes us or we finish this. We have nowhere else to turn. You know about magic and spirits. We need your help. I'm afraid we're all going to die without your help."

Silence fell over the clearing. Paula and Larry looked at each other, then back at the house. Paula started to call out again, but the front door creaked open. A frail old man stepped out onto the porch. He wore dingy, stained overalls and a yellowed thermal shirt. A thick white beard framed his face then faded into patchy whisps on his head. He held a shotgun in one hand, but it was pointed downward, the barrel resting on the porch as more of a cane than a weapon.

"I remember you," Crenshaw said. "Your daddy was glad you got away before that bitch could get you. Why the hell'd you come back?"

"A funeral," Paula replied.

"Gonna be your own."

"That's what we're trying to stop," Larry said.

"Try all you want, but ain't much can stop that damn witch."

"A witch?"

"Not like you're thinkin. She ain't ridin' no broomstick. She's a devil is what she is."

"The—*thing* we keep seeing?" Larry asked.

"Yellow eyes, snake tongue, fingers long as tree branches?"

"Yes," Paula and Larry said in unison.

"That's her alright. If you're gonna call on the mountain spirits, she ain't the one you want answering. Witch, demon, devil, evil spirit. Don't matter what you call her. She's a vengeful, nasty thing. No offense to you, miss, but your daddy fucked up when he asked her for help. And now here you are, stirring her back up. I oughta run you off this mountain before you bring her this way. She knows better than to trifle with me—I got a few tricks up my sleeve, and she knows it—but all the same, I'd rather not have to fuss with her."

"That's why we're here. Those tricks up your sleeve. We need to find a way to send her back to wherever the hell she came from." Larry paused and stared at the old man. "I can't let anything else happen to these girls."

Angie got out of the car and stepped up next to Paula.

"Please, Mr. Crenshaw. If you won't help us, no one can."

The old man sighed. He scanned the trio of visitors and then looked around the clearing. "Y'all are good folks caught up in something never should've happened. You have my sympathies. I can't make any guarantees. There are no guarantees in this business. There's only one way I know to end a thing like this, and you won't be happy about what needs to be done, but it's the only way."

"Whatever it is, we'll do it." Larry said. "Like I said, I can't let anything else happen to these girls."

"That there is the problem. If you want to stop that bitch, one of you is gonna have to die."

CHAPTER 22

Crenshaw stared at them. "I'll tell you what I know, and you can decide if you want to walk the path or not. Makes no difference to me." He turned and walked back inside the shack.

"I don't believe this," Angie said. She ran her fingers through her hair and leaned her head back, staring at the sky.

"Let's hear what he has to say, and then we'll decide what we'll do. I'm not ready to call it off," Larry said.

"It's too late for that, anyway," Paula said. "If we don't move ahead, I think we'll all be dead soon. Let's hear him out."

Angie moaned. "Fine. You're right. I hate it, but you're right."

Larry nodded and led the girls on to the porch. The wood creaked and sagged with each step, but managed to hold. He stood by the door, unsure if he should knock, but Crenshaw called from inside.

"Come on if you're coming."

They stepped into a room filled with shadows. An unpleasant odor permeated the air—something akin to old meat. Crenshaw sat on a wooden chair placed in the corner of the room. Several weathered books were spread on a table next to him. The fire burnt low, casting dim orange light into the room.

"You mind?" Crenshaw asked, pointing at a small stack of split logs near the fireplace.

Larry grunted and stacked two pieces into the fire. The wood caught quickly. In the brighter glow, Larry saw several unusual idols and trinkets scattered about the room. "Nice place you've got here, Albert."

Crenshaw snorted. "Don't mock me. I ain't the one needing help."

"Didn't mean to offend."

"I would hope not."

"So," Paula said, interrupting the tension between the two men, "what can you tell us about this *bitch* as you call her. Maybe start by telling us what exactly my father did. If we know what mistakes he made, maybe we can avoid doing the same thing."

"Calling her at all was his first mistake. What your daddy was out to do is no easy thing. There's a balance to this world. Life and death. Both are natural things. The natural world is much more than most folks give it credit for. Lot of folks don't believe in things they can't see, or don't believe the things they *do* see when it doesn't suit 'em. The world is a living, breathing *being*. It's much more than this rock we call Earth. So much more."

"You're talking about spirits and demons and such, right?" Larry asked.

"And such. It's not that simple. There are many planes of existence, both physical and spiritual. These places are home to beings of endless kinds. Some good, some bad, some indifferent. These places can overlap and collide. There are doors to other places, if you know where to find them. Sometimes they come and go. Sometimes they can be left open. All this exists together and separately at the same time."

"Alternate dimensions," Paula said.

"That's one name for it," Crenshaw replied. "The beings that inhabit these other places, they can come through into other planes. Might be because they want to. Other times, they can be called. There are ways to do that. People like me know how. I hear folks call it magic. That's fine, I guess. No tricks to it, though. The energy is all around us, all the time. Just have to know how to use it."

"My dad asked you to use this energy to save my mother."

"He did. It's a lot to ask, and I tried to change his mind, but he was set on his path. Now, I didn't send him out into those woods with the idea of calling on an evil spirit for aid. Like I said, spirits can be good, bad, or indifferent. Most *are* indifferent. The bad ones tend to be the easiest to find. They're mischievous. Looking to deceive and cause torment. Your daddy went out there, made an offering, and called for help. He was terribly unlucky in who answered his call. I wasn't there. I can't say what was promised. I'm sure she lied, told him she could save your momma. My guess is she made him swear himself to her, without telling him what that means."

"What's it mean?"

"If you swear yourself to a demon like her, it means you give all your essence, both in this life and the next, to her service. Essence runs in the blood, and blood runs through the family."

Paula's face paled. "So he swore his whole family to a demon, which included me and my brother."

"Afraid so," Crenshaw said. "The demon lied about saving your mother, probably through some trickery. They are deceitful and manipulative. No evil spirit will offer genuine help. It's not their nature."

"So what can we do to end this?" Larry asked, pacing circles around the room. "How can we break this *deal?*"

"I don't think you can break it. Never known a spirit to dissolve a deal. I don't know how to break it, but I know how to end it."

"What's the difference?" Larry stopped pacing and glared at the old man.

"Finalize the deal." Crenshaw turned to Paula. "You have no children?"

"No."

"Then the essence ends with you. Once the spirit claims you, the deal is fulfilled and the spirit will have no claim to meddle any further. If you want to end this, you'll have to give yourself over." Crenshaw paused, pulled a tobacco pouch from his pocket, and pushed a wad into his mouth. His cheek swelled and he spit into a metal bucket beside the chair. "I told you you wouldn't like it."

"Nope," Larry said, nearly shouting. "There's another way. Has to be another way."

Angie slumped against the wall and closed her eyes. Paula stared at the blazing fire.

"C'mon, girls," Larry pleaded. "Don't quit on me now. We're going to find another way."

"It makes sense," Paula said. "If my father made this deal, it should end with me."

"But we don't *know* that was the deal. He said it himself, he wasn't there."

"True enough," Crenshaw replied. "I wasn't there. But, I've seen enough to read the signs. Y'all are free to try whatever you like. A warning though, and don't take this lightly." Crenshaw leaned forward in his chair, waiting until he had the full attention of the room. "Do not try to deal with the devil. Your daddy tried and you see what it got him, and what it got you. Y'all are in a bad way, and there ain't no easy way out. Don't make it worse on yourselves." Crenshaw started to say more, then stopped abruptly, his eyes shifting to the front window. He frowned and launched another stream of brown spit into the bucket. "I wish you well and hope you find peace, but it's time for y'all to go. The shadows that trail you are catching up, and I'd just as soon they not trespass on my property."

"I feel it, too," Paula said. She shifted her eyes to the window and back. "We need to go."

"Okay," Larry said. He stopped and looked back at Crenshaw. "I'm going to prove you wrong."

"I hope you do."

CHAPTER 23

Night had fallen when Angie's headlights illuminated the house. No one spoke as they exited the car and filed into the kitchen, flipping on lights. Whiskers was where they'd left him, curled up on the blanket. He blinked at the sudden illumination, scrunched his nose in a display of annoyance, then went back to sleep. A suffocating melancholy hung in the air, and no one was quick to speak. Paula hadn't said a word since leaving Crenshaw's place. Her eyes were empty, her thoughts miles away. Larry collapsed into a kitchen chair and slumped his shoulders. Angie's heart ached, both for what seemed to be coming and the despair in her father's eyes. Unable to bear the silence any longer, she cleared her throat and spoke.

"What are we going to do?"

"I think I should go alone," Paula said.

"No!" Larry's outburst shook both girls.

"I'm sorry, Uncle Larry. If this is how it's going to end, there's no sense in putting you two in danger. It wants me, and this will be over when it's done."

"Listen to yourself, girl. You can't ask this of us. I can't let you walk into those woods to your death or worse."

"He's right, Paula. We know it's dangerous, but we also don't know if this is truly the only way. I think if there's a chance, we'll find it together. You going out there alone is giving up. I'm not ready to do that."

"Me neither," Larry said.

Paula wiped her eyes. "And I love you both for it. See it from my side. Think about how much you don't want anything bad to happen to me. That's how I feel about you, and the difference is I can actually keep you two from harm. I'm scared to death to go out there alone, but I'm more scared of letting something happen to you when I can stop it."

"I understand you, Paula, I really do, but it doesn't matter. We're family, and we will face this together," Larry said. "I'll die before I let you go alone."

Paula sobbed. "You'll die if you don't!"

"You don't know that."

"We're coming with you, no matter what, so stop arguing with us. Let's decide exactly *what* we're going to do," Angie said. "What's your plan?"

Paula laughed through her tears, a broken noise. "Well, it was just to go to the cemetery and see what happens."

Angie stared at her incredulously, then snorted a laugh of her own. "Good plan."

"Ridiculous as it sounds, I think that's where we start," Larry said. "I have every reason to believe this God forsaken thing can hear us, or at least sense what we're thinking. My gut says it'll be waiting in the cemetery."

"At the fire," Angie said. She shivered.

"I suspect so. But before we go, we should arm ourselves."

"Dad, guns and knives aren't going to help us here."

"That's not what I mean," Larry said. He stood and exited the kitchen, thumping away through the house. When he returned a moment later, he held three crucifix necklaces in his hand, each of varying size and design. He held up the first, the smallest, secured on a thin silver chain. "This was my mother's. Ang, I've been meaning to give this to you for a long time, but it always seems to slip my mind." He reached out and dropped the necklace onto Angie's outstretched palm. "This one, Paula, belonged to Candy. I planned to give it to you before you left after the funeral, but I forgot. Kicked myself for it, too, since at the time I wasn't sure when I'd see you again. It was important to me that you have it, and I couldn't believe I forgot. Now, I'm starting to think me holding onto these was by design. Maybe, I was supposed to keep them until you needed them." He handed Candy's crucifix, this one gold with a matching chain, to Paula. He held up the remaining necklace, a thick silver cross tarnished with age. "This one belonged to my grandad, and it was passed down to him. I don't know exactly how old it is, but I know it's the oldest thing I own. There's power in that. Old faith. We'll need that tonight. You girls may be skeptical, but I believe. Humor an old man, and wear these."

Both girls nodded. Angie's necklace chain was long, and she slipped it easily over her head. Paula had to unclasp the hook on hers and wrap it around her neck. Larry followed suit, securing the chain around his own neck. He crossed the kitchen, and pulled a small toolbox from underneath the sink. Inside, he retrieved a large, heavy-duty flashlight. "This is the only one we got, so if it wasn't already obvious, we need to stay together."

Angie exhaled. "Let's get this over with."

Paula nodded, then hugged them both. "Whatever happens, I'm glad I got to spend time with you guys again. It's been nice to know what family feels like. Real family."

Larry squeezed her gently, then cleared the lump from his throat. "This won't be the last time. Have faith in that."

Angie took Paula's hand and led her outside. The night air was cool and the sky dark. Night sounds floated on the breeze. It would have been peaceful under other circumstances.

The three of them crossed the dark lawn, the flashlight beam bobbing a path in front of them. The image sent Larry back to the night of the funeral, watching a similar scene from his bedroom window. If only he'd followed his instincts then, stopped them from going. Maybe none of this would have happened. But the thought rang false in his mind. This was inevitable—events set in motion years ago by a desperate man.

They reached the tree line and paused. Larry handed the flashlight to Angie, then took both girls by the hand. "Stay together and have faith. If there's a way to end this and come out the other side, we're going to find it. I love you girls with all my heart."

"I love you, too, Dad."

"I love you, Uncle Larry."

"God willing, that's enough to see us through."

The forest stood waiting. Hand-in-hand, they stepped inside.

CHAPTER 24

The trees closed in around them. Angie's breath quickened and she fought a wave of panic. *Breathe, girl, breathe.*

"Why do I have to go first?"

"You know the way better than I do," Larry said. He squeezed her hand. "I'm right behind you."

Angie nodded. He was right. The light swayed over the narrow path in the forest floor. She kept her focus straight ahead, alternating from the ground to the landscape ahead and back, careful not to trip or get off track, but also intentionally avoiding letting her gaze drift to the trees. Eyes were upon them, and she was terrified to look back.

They traveled cautiously but without hesitation deeper into the trees. Angie waited for a whisper, a face, anything, but nothing came aside from the steady crunch of their steps. *It has no reason to stop us. We're not running away this time. We're going to it.*

"Wait," Paula said, breaking the silence. "This doesn't feel right."

"What doesn't feel right?" Larry asked.

"I feel like we're going the wrong way."

"This is how we went last time," Angie said. "There's only one path, and we're still on it. See?" Angie turned and shined the flashlight beam at the ground. "What the hell?"

Six feet ahead, the path branched into two different directions. Both paths were identical, narrow roads worn into the dirt.

"This was never here," Angie said, panic rising. "It's always been one path."

"It's messing with us," Paula said.

Laughter echoed through the trees, and Angie moaned.

Larry pulled her to him. "Why the trickery?" he shouted. "We're coming to you. If you have nothing to fear from us, then why slow us down?" Larry turned to Paula and lowered his voice. "I'll tell you why. Because this isn't a sure thing. If we were walking to our doom, it wouldn't stop us. It's trying to confuse us. Why? Because it's afraid, that's why. Angie, which way feels right?"

Angie shined the light back and forth between the two paths, then stopped on the right. "It's this way. It's uphill the closer you get to the cemetery, not down."

"Right it is. Keep moving."

They pressed on into the darkness. The path started a gradual incline. Whispers pierced the buzz and chirp of insects—unintelligible, foreign, and out of place amongst the forest sounds. Branches snapped and tree tops rustled as if something large moved through them, hopping from tree to tree.

Don't look up, Angie thought. She strained to hear the dry whispers and wondered if Paula or her dad could make out any words. They'd fallen silent behind her. Angie slowed. Her crunching steps were no longer accompanied by two more sets of feet. She froze and silence engulfed her. Even the crickets paused their song. A sudden wind sent the dark canopy into a flutter, whipping leaves from the trees. Angie turned back, knowing what she would find.

She was alone. The flashlight illuminated the path a dozen feet, but the trail was empty.

"DAD! PAULA!"

The night swallowed her screams. Her heartbeat skyrocketed and nausea racked her stomach. Tears filled her eyes and she screamed again. "DAD!"

"Hello, Angie. Are you lost?"

Angie stiffened and felt faint—her blood like ice coursing through her veins. The voice behind her was impossible, but she knew it well.

"Could you check my vitals, dear? I'm afraid I might be terribly ill."

She turned back up the trail, dragging the light beam with her until it found him.

Mr. Leshner stood a dozen feet up the trail. He was naked—rib cage swelling against his sagging yellow skin, thin arms dangling at his sides. Despite his withered and frail state, his erect penis jutted from a wispy thatch of gray pubic hair.

Bile filled Angie's throat, and she gagged.

"I told you I'd have you, Angie." He grinned and tugged himself. "I'll take you here and then take you into the fire. You'll be mine to spoil, over and again, forever." He shambled forward. "Nurse, I need your services. It seems my glands are swollen." He let out an ugly, offensive cackle. Another step. "I've been waiting for you. *We* have been waiting." Another step. He ran his pale tongue over cracked lips, then launched himself at her in a staggering run.

Angie shrieked and dove to the side. His fingers grazed her shirt but didn't grab hold. She scrambled to her feet and raced into the trees, no longer caring about the path. She couldn't hear if he was chasing her or how close he might be, but looking back was not an option. Her chest burned and a painful stitch in her side stabbed with every step, but she pushed onward. Nothing around her looked familiar and only trees and darkness lay before her. Nearing collapse, she grabbed the nearest tree and looped around behind it, twisting the flashlight into the woods behind her.

Nothing.

She sobbed and dropped to her knees, gasping for air. *Hide,* she thought. *Can't run anymore. Have to hide.* She snapped off the flashlight, plunging herself into absolute darkness, and pulled her knees against her chest, shrinking herself as tightly as she could into the base of the tree. She closed her eyes and buried her head into her knees, desperately trying to stay quiet.

In the dark, she waited and prayed.

CHAPTER 25

"Did you hear that?" Larry stopped and turned. Paula bumped into him and he put his hands up to brace her. "Listen."

Paula slowed her breath and closed her eyes to focus, but heard only the soft rustling of leaves on the wind.

"I don't hear anything," she whispered.

"Someone called my name. Back the way we came, but far away. Maybe even from the yard." Larry paused, listened, and then snapped his head back down the trail. "There! You heard that, right? I know that voice, but I can't place it."

Paula frowned. "I didn't hear it."

"Angie, you heard it, didn't you? Angie?"

Paula turned to find the trail ahead cloaked in darkness, and her stomach dropped.

"Angie, why'd you turn off the light?" Larry asked, his voice quivering with uncertainty. "Angie?"

"She's gone," Paula said, her voice barely audible.

"ANGIE!" Larry's voice roared through the trees. "ANGIE!"

Larry launched into a blind run further down the dark path.

"Wait!"

Larry ignored her call, his silhouette shrinking as the distance between them increased. Desperate not to lose him, Paula forced her feet into action and ran after him.

"ANGIE, WHERE ARE YOU?!"

His shouts gave her direction, but she couldn't see; she was chasing sound. She had not thought the woods could possibly be any darker, but the deeper they went, the thicker the blackness.

"LARRY, WAIT FOR ME!" Paula's voice cracked. A short time ago she'd wanted to make this journey alone, but now she couldn't bear the thought of facing this without Larry and Angie. "PLEASE! LARRY!"

Larry didn't reply. He no longer shouted for Angie either. His silence struck a deeper fear in Paula's heart. She was isolated and vulnerable. Her fear urged her to abort the mission, try to make it back to Larry's house, but she knew it was hopeless. It was unlikely she could find her way back in the dark, and she knew escaping the woods did not mean escaping her fate. This thing would find her wherever she went.

Nearing collapse, she pushed through a thick patch of bushes and saw the outline of a figure ahead, standing still. She blew out an exhale of relief.

"Larry, please wait for me."

She stumbled through the dark, closing the distance, and grabbed onto his arm. "Larry?"

Larry stood rigid and motionless, staring straight ahead. Paula followed his frozen gaze and stiffened. Another figure stood further down the path, cloaked in shadow.

"Angie?" Paula called out.

"Not her," Larry said.

Buried within the shadowy figure, yellow eyes blinked.

"What have you done with her?" Larry said, his voice steady, betraying no emotion. "My daughter, what have you done with her?"

The thing continued to blink, but made no sound.

"Where is she?"

Softly, a voice drifted across the wood. "Do you fancy a trade?" The voice was delicate and melodic, not at all what Paula anticipated.

"I'll have my daughter back, and I'll send you back to the pits of Hell."

"You know nothing of Hell, but test me, and you will."

"I'm not afraid of you," Larry said.

"You should be," the voice said. "What you have witnessed is child's play. What your daughter will soon witness is beyond your imagination. But it does not have to be. I was promised a soul I've yet to claim. Stand in my way, and I'll take it along with yours and your daughter's. You will spend eternity bearing witness to debauchery and the defiling of your child. Do not doubt me. Stand aside, give me the soul agreed upon, and you and your child will leave these woods with your souls intact."

"Larry." Paula took his hand and squeezed it gently. "This is how it has to be. I won't let you suffer for me."

"Bullshit," Larry said. "This is not over. Why try to deal with me? Why not take us all? Because it can't. Because it's afraid of something."

"Your confidence is misplaced and futile. I fear nothing. I *am* fear."

"Then come and get me you bitch!"

The jingle of laughter surrounded them and Paula screamed. The figure dashed forward toward them, its cracked face coming into focus, exposing serrated teeth. Larry grabbed Paula by the shoulder and shoved her away. She was not prepared and tumbled down into a tangle of vines and twigs.

Larry roared in defiance and collided with the figure. Despite his considerable size, he was driven sharply backward, lifted off his feet, and slammed onto the ground. He groaned in protest, but rolled to his side, scrambling back to his feet. Paula struggled to stand, but something pulled her back. She stared in horror as vines wrapped and twisted around her limbs, digging into her skin, thorns piercing and drawing blood. A scream tore from her throat, but she could not free herself.

The figure flashed through the trees around them, and Larry twisted wildly, arms raised in defense, waiting for the next attack. It swooped in again, this time knocking him sideways, but not hard enough to drop him. He righted himself, then locked eyes on the figure, which now stood motionless ten feet away.

"Her screams will torment you forever, and there's nothing you can do to save her."

Larry bellowed an echoing roar and charged the figure. Its yellow eyes flashed and at the moment of impact, it twisted to the side, grabbed Larry by the arm and flung him into a tree. A sickening crunch sounded, and Larry groaned in agony. He staggered backwards, hands clutching his stomach. A thick, jagged branch protruded from the tree in front of him. Even in the dark, he could see red ooze and meat clinging to it. He looked down, then his legs gave out.

Paula shrieked. The vines relaxed and fell loose. She crawled to Larry and cried out. The wound was worse than it appeared from a distance. Blood pooled and surged sending red streams down his stomach and onto the forest floor.

"Hold on, Larry," she said through tears. "Just hold on."

He met her eyes but couldn't speak, gasping ragged, wet breaths.

"I'm going to end this, and Angie's going to be okay. I promise."

The dark shape of the thing approached. She pushed to her feet and stared back with burning hatred. "Let's end this. I will complete the deal my father made, but you will not hurt him or Angie again. Are we clear?"

"I have already agreed to those terms. Now come."

The figure turned and floated away down the path. Paula followed.

CHAPTER 26

Time lost meaning for Angie. She had no idea how long she'd been crouched behind the tree. It felt like hours had passed. Realistically, she knew it could not have been more than fifteen or twenty minutes. The only thing she knew for sure was Mr. Leshner had not found her, and she had not heard any sound except crickets for some time. Her knees and hamstrings ached from squatting, and after several excruciating minutes, she'd allowed herself to drop onto her butt and relieve the tension. She knew it put her at a disadvantage in the event she needed to get up and run quickly, but the burning in her legs was too much.

She fought the urge to relax. It was impossible to believe Mr. Leshner gave up his search. Many nights watching horror movies taught her that, when she did stand up, Mr. Leshner would be standing just on the other side of the tree, waiting. This fear held her in place, but she was almost equally scared to stay put. Her dad and Paula were still out there, and they had to be in trouble. Shame and guilt racked her.

What are you going to do? Sit here and wait until that pervy old bastard finds you while Dad and Paula try to save us all? Grow a backbone and fight!

She knew the voice was right. Her options were to stay here and wait for whatever horrible thing may come, or get up and fight.

Get up and fight.

She mouthed the words as she thought them, then whispered them aloud.

"Get up and fight."

Harnessing her sudden courage, she pushed off the forest floor, ignoring the ache in her legs, and sidestepped quickly away from the tree. To her profound relief, Mr. Leshner was not waiting for her. The crickets chirped as if nothing strange had transpired. She walked slowly back the way she'd come. She flipped on the flashlight, and the illumination revealed the trail a few feet away. Trusting her sense of direction, she rejoined the path and headed to the right. As her mind cleared, she estimated she'd run maybe a half mile. There was no guarantee Dad and Paula would be where she left them, but it was the best place to start.

She quietly called out to them. Screaming into the forest was just as likely to draw attention she didn't want.

"Dad? Paula? Can you hear me?"

No answer. It was a bittersweet silence. Her heart ached to hear them call back, but everytime she didn't hear Mr. Leshner's croaking voice was a relief.

Something felt different now. The atmosphere had changed. From the moment they stepped into the trees, the air was thick with tension. Now, it was lighter. She no longer felt the constant pressing of being watched. Maybe Dad and Paula found a way to end this. It was wishful thinking, but something had changed.

The path curved sharply through a thick patch of trees, and Angie called out once more. "Can you guys hear me?"

A low moan, barely audible, came from her left and she froze, slashing the light across the trees, bracing herself for whatever she might find. The path continued that direction, slowly sloping up an incline, but she saw no one.

"Hello?"

"Mmmmmm," came the moan again, weaker this time.

She crept in the direction of the sound.

"Dad? Paula?"

A branch snapped to her right, and she spun.

Larry lay on the ground next to a tree. His shirt was stained red and his skin was ghostly pale. He held a branch in his hand, and whacked the tree with it again. His mouth opened as if he were trying to call for her, but his voice failed.

"Oh my God, Dad!" Angie ran to him and dropped to his side. She'd seen many dying people during her time at the office and the hospital. It didn't take a nurse to know he had lost too much blood. "Jesus, what happened? Where's Paula?"

Larry's eyes were wide and glazed. Short, wheezing gasps escaped his lips as he tried to speak. He pointed the branch in his hand toward the trail. "Gone.....with....."

"With the...demon?"

Larry nodded and dropped his arm back to the ground. "Couldn't... stop her." He coughed and a spray of red misted the air. "Thought I....lost...you, too. Are you...okay?"

"I'm fine, Dad." She looked around helplessly. "We've got to stop your bleeding, okay?"

"Too late," Larry said weakly. "Go help...Paula."

"I will, but I'm gonna help you first." She sucked in a deep breath to clear her nerves, then quickly pulled her hoodie over head. She folded it over and placed it over his stomach. "I'm gonna take your belt off. Help me out, here." She unhooked his belt and pulled, but it held firm in the loops of his jeans. "Lean with me."

Larry leaned to his side and cried out in pain, but the shift in weight was enough to allow Angie to yank the belt free.

"Stay on your side," she instructed, then fed the belt under his back. "I know it hurts, but I need you to lean the other way now so I can wrap the belt around you."

Larry nodded, gritted his teeth, and rolled back to the other side. This time he roared, launching a coughing fit sending more blood spray misting onto the ground.

"Okay, now lay back and be still." She pulled the belt through the clasp and lined it up over the sweatshirt. "This part is gonna hurt, too, but it has to be tight."

"Do it," Larry groaned.

Angie nodded and pulled the belt as tight as she could, cinching it across his midsection. He grimaced, but stayed silent. "That's the best I can do right now. I'm gonna go, okay. I'm gonna find Paula, and we're all getting out of here."

"I love you...Ang."

"I love you, too, Dad," Angie said through tears, "but this is not goodbye. Do you understand me?"

Larry nodded, but she saw the truth in his eyes.

"I'll be back."

She stood quickly, before she could change her mind, and sprinted up the path.

Please, God, don't let it be too late.

CHAPTER 27

Paula walked through the forest in a daze. A million thoughts drifted through her mind, but she was unable to focus on anything other than the figure drifting along in front of her. No words passed between them. None were needed. This was the end.

As she walked her final steps, she realized the futility of their campaign to fight back against the demon. From the moment she walked into the woods that first night with Angie, her fate was sealed. Evil had been waiting for her to return home. She wondered how long it would have taken for the demon to seek her out, had she not returned on her own. It was inevitable. A deal was a deal, and her father, well intentioned as he was, signed all their names in blood.

Her only remaining hope was that the demon would be true to its word and leave Larry and Angie alone, if it wasn't already too late for them both. For all she knew, Angie was dead already, and Larry would bleed to death if help didn't come soon. Part of her wanted to question the demon, but she feared mentioning them at this point would only tempt the creature. Crenshaw was insistent about the demon's deceitful nature. No good would come from asking, and she wanted to spend her last few minutes with the hope things would be okay for her family, naive as that might be.

The sky slowly brightened. Paula recognized the orange glow. The cemetery was near and the fire burned once more. A moment later, she stood at the hilltop where she'd crawled to the edge, Angie at her side, only a few short days before. The cemetery was engulfed in shimmering light. Dark figures stood motionless around the burning tree. The demon drifted down the hillside, and Paula followed, resigned to whatever horrors awaited. The heat radiating from the fire pressed against her. *This is hell. I'm walking into hell.*

The demon reached the bottom and crossed into the cemetery proper. It entered the loose circle formed by the shadowy figures around the tree, then stopped. "Come," it hissed. "Join your family."

Paula slid the last few feet down the hillside, nearly toppling over, but managed to stay on her feet. The figures in the cemetery wore black robes with hoods pulled over their heads.

"A long past-due family reunion," said the demon. It turned, facing Paula for the first time since they'd left Larry bleeding in the woods, and smiled. The pale tongue slithered out, flicked at the air and withdrew once more. "Don't be shy. Show yourselves to our visitor. She'll be so happy to see you all again."

The three figures nearest Paula lifted their arms in unison and pushed the hoods back. Paula stepped forward, bracing for what she knew she would see. She turned to the first and her knees buckled, dropping her to the cemetery floor.

"No, mama," she moaned.

The face staring back at her was scarred and mangled, but Paula would know it anywhere. Black vines with vicious, jagged thorns wrapped her mother from head to toe, sealing her mouth and binding her arms and legs together. Her eyes were blank, void of any consciousness or understanding.

Unable to stop herself, she turned her eyes to the next figure. Her father wore chains, shackling his hands behind his back, tethering them to chains around his ankles. Unlike her mother, his eyes were wide and wild, locked on her in despair. The chains rattled as he bucked against them, but it was a useless effort. He thrashed his head back and forth. His intention was clear. He wanted her to run.

Paula was struck by how *real* they looked. Her parents were dead, yet they looked like living, breathing flesh and blood. They existed in more than a spiritual sense. She knew if she reached out and touched them, she would feel a physical being—tortured and tormented physical beings.

A third figure stood further down the line, and her brother's face nearly broke her. Unlike her parents, he did not appear to be bound. His arms hung loosely at his sides, and he stared straight ahead at the fire, seemingly paying no mind to the events unfolding nearby.

"Lonny?" Paula's voice cracked as she spoke his name.

He turned toward her and their eyes met. A sadness gripped his features and after a moment, his gaze slipped from her and turned back to the fire.

"I thought I might bind you two together. Siblings lost to a father's misfortune."

"Why?"

"Why not? You are all mine. I delight in your simple suffering."

"No," Paula said. She stood and turned defiantly to the demon. "Why show me this at all? Why not just take me?"

"Are you eager to suffer?"

"What are you waiting for?"

The demon snarled and snapped its tongue into the air again. "Cast aside your earthly possessions and step into the fire."

Earthly possessions? Paula's brow furrowed as she considered. She held nothing in her hands, and her pockets were empty. A gentle breeze touched her, cooling air against the fire's heat, carrying a pronounced scent of honeysuckle. The scent brought with it a memory—Aunt Candace wrapping her up in a hug on her front porch all those years ago. A cold weight pressed against her chest, and she pressed her hand against it, feeling the crucifix necklace, cool to the touch. *Candy's crucifix.*

Energy coursed through her veins. Her fear faded, replaced by a confidence she'd thought lost. The demon sneered at her and drifted back. Paula turned toward her family, clutching the crucifix in her hand. Her father nodded vigorously. Lonny cocked his head and raised an eyebrow. It was a gesture she'd seen a thousand times—a sly look to secretly encourage her when she was about to do something mischievous. Her mother still stared straight ahead, eyes vacant and empty, but Paula saw the faintest twitch at the corner of her mouth, teasing the smallest of smiles.

"Cast it aside and step to the fire," the demon growled.

"This?" Paula asked. She lifted the crucifix into the air. "You worried about this?"

"Your faith means nothing. Your God is not here."

"Then why are you backing away?"

"Cast it aside, girl. I've spared your brother so you may suffer together. Test me and you shall bear witness to his binding. Your faith will not save you."

"You're right," Paula said. "My faith won't save me." She removed the necklace and held it out, flames flashing off the metal. "I lost my faith a long time ago, and maybe I can't get it back. But that's okay. Aunt Candy has enough for both of us."

Paula charged across the cemetery, let the crucifix drop, kept her fingers coiled around the chain, and swung it at the demon in a wide arc. The crucifix slashed across its face and a high pitched shriek echoed across the cemetery. The burning tree erupted, flames reaching higher into the night. The demon shifted away from her, floating across the grass, but it moved in slow, jerky motions. Paula closed the distance and swung the chain again, this time the crucifix slashing across the demon's back. Another screech of pain filled the air, and the flames surged again. The demon fell forward and collapsed.

Paula watched the creature as it tried to crawl away, tongue dragging the ground. Its yellow eyes darted back and forth from her to the fire. The flames roared higher, heat singeing her hair, but Paula resisted. She slashed again and the demon howled. Its arms gave out and it lay motionless on the ground, save for the pale tongue flicking at the dirt. She turned her back on the demon and looked to her family. Lonny smiled coyly, and stepped over to their father. He grabbed the chains binding him and they dropped in a heap at his feet. Her father lifted a hand, pressed it to his lips, and held it out to her. Lonny moved on to their mother and repeated the ritual. The vines binding her loosened and fell away. Her eyes cleared and she looked around the cemetery in a daze, as if awaking from a terrible dream. She looked at Lonny, then at Paula. Understanding crossed her face and she smiled. Lonny took her hand, then turned and reached out to their father. Her father looked once more to Paula, nodded and took Lonny's hand. Then they were gone.

Paula dropped to her knees, her cheeks glistening with tears. The demon let out a whimpering moan from behind her. *Finish it*, she thought. It was getting harder to see, and she realized it wasn't only because of her tears. The fire was fading, the night creeping back into the cemetery. She struggled to her feet and prepared to cast a final blow, but motion in the trees caught her eye.

Angie stepped into the fading light. She sprinted across the cemetery and threw her arms around Paula.

"You did it! I don't believe it. How?"

Paula squeezed back, clinging to her. "The crucifix. Candy's crucifix." She pushed away and looked Angie in the face. "She was here. Candy. She was here," Paula said, holding the crucifix up for Angie to see.

Angie removed her own crucifix and stepped up beside the demon.

"This is for my Dad, you bitch."

The demon's yellow eyes darted up at Angie's face and it clamped its hand around her ankle. Angie screamed and slashed the crucifix at the creature.

An unearthly shriek echoed into the night and the cemetery fell into darkness.

The girls walked as quickly as they could manage. Angie limped along, favoring her ankle that bore a laceration from the demon's claw. The wound stung with each step, but it wasn't deep and the bleeding was minimal. The climb up the hill was particularly painful, but she made it without much issue. She pressed herself as hard as she could, knowing full well time was not on their side, if it hadn't already run out. She prayed it had not.

The trail carried on through the woods as it always had. The new paths and branches created by the demon were gone. Everything about the woods felt renewed. The tainted energy cast by the demon was no more.

"Just down there, around that bend," Angie said. "That's where he was."

They picked up their pace, Angie ignoring the fresh bursts of tenderness from her ankle, and emerged into the small clearing. She scanned the flashlight beam across from left to right and her stomach dropped.

"He was right there," Paula said, pointing across the clearing.

"I know. He was there when I left him, too."

"Could he have been able to walk?" Paula asked.

"I don't know. I don't think so. What if that thing took him?"

Angie turned to Paula, her eyes wide with fear. "Paula, what if it took him?"

Paula sighed. "I don't know how, Angie. We killed it."

"Dad!" Angie shouted, cupping her hands around her mouth. "Where are you?"

Paula took the flashlight from Angie and carried it to the spot where Larry had been. The grass was stained red.

"Angie, come here."

Angie hobbled over and looked at the ground. Bloody streaks led away, further up the trail.

"Follow it," Angie said, then shouted again. "Dad!"

They walked slowly, careful not to lose the trail. The blood came in patches, sometimes skipping a few feet. He'd clearly crawled away—or been dragged.

"Larry!"

"Dad!"

Their calls echoed through the trees. Angie knew they were nearing the wood's edge where it would open up to the backyard. She almost stopped and suggested they double back when a low moan came from her right. She pivoted and slashed the flashlight into the trees. Larry lay a few feet off the trail, mud and leaves matted to his body with blood. His skin was shockingly white, but his eyes were open and he stared up at her with obvious relief.

"Girls," he whispered. "Is it...over?"

Angie rushed to his side and dropped to her knees. She took his hands in hers and winced at the coldness of his touch. She pressed her fingers into his wrist and felt for his pulse. It was weak and slow, but steady.

"Paula, take the flashlight. Follow the trail back out, it's not much farther. Get to the house and call an ambulance. Hurry."

Paula nodded and sprinted down the trail, vanishing from sight, leaving Angie and Larry in darkness.

"It's over, Dad. We killed it. We sent it back to whatever hell it came from."

"Are...you...sure?"

"Sure as I can be. Don't worry about it, now. Just relax and be still. You should've stayed put."

"I was...trying to get...back. Call for...help."

"Help is on the way. Stay with me, old man. I'm too reckless to have no supervision."

Larry chuckled, then groaned. "Don't make me laugh. It...hurts."

Angie adjusted the belt wrapped around his stomach. It slipped low during his crawling escape, and she cinched it tight again. Then, she held his hand and lay down on the ground beside him.

"I told you it wasn't goodbye."

Larry squeezed her hand, albeit weakly, and they lay together in silence.

Moments later, footfalls crunched in the foliage as Paula jogged back to them. The light beam illuminated the trail, and Paula stumbled to a stop beside them. She pointed the light at Larry. His eyes were closed, but his chest continued to rise and fall in slow shallow breaths.

"They're coming. Is he okay?"

"I think so. I hope so," Angie said. "I'm not ready to let him go."

"Me neither," Paula replied. She squatted and sat next to Angie.

"What are we going to tell them?" Angie asked.

"Who?"

"The paramedics, police, whoever shows up."

"That Larry got hurt helping us fight a demon so we could free our family from eternal torment?"

Angie cracked a smile, then a laugh escaped her lips. Paula joined in, and the two spiraled into hysterics, giggling like children. The nocturnal forest creatures chirped along with them, and down the mountain a siren wailed.

"Go on, Paula. They're coming. You'll need to direct them back here. Tell them they'll have to carry him out. A stretcher isn't gonna roll back here. I'll stay with Dad."

Paula stood and jogged away. Angie checked his pulse and respirations again. Still slow but steady. She listened as the siren call approached, then cut off with a single *WHOOP*. Voices floated in the air, and soon she heard the approaching footsteps.

For the first time in what felt like a very long time, she let herself relax.

Everything was going to be okay.

CHAPTER 29

"Why are we doing this?" Angie asked.

Paula stared ahead through the windshield. Truthfully, she didn't have a good answer for that. It just felt like the thing to do.

"I think it's important."

"Why? Haven't you had enough spooky shit?"

"Enough for a lifetime, but if this happened to us, it could happen to someone else. I'll feel better if I pass along what I know."

"I guess," Angie said. "But it's not like he's listed in the phonebook under demon slaying services. Only people around here even know who he is."

"I know," Paula replied. "You didn't have to come. In fact, I told you to stay with your dad."

Angie rolled her eyes. "Neither one of us was gonna be okay with you going out here by yourself. I'm sorry to complain. I just want to put this behind us."

"We will. I know you don't want to be here, but I'm glad you're with me," Paula said.

"Me going with you means you have to let me come spend a weekend with you in Ohio soon."

Paula smiled. "Absolutely."

They traveled the rest of the narrow mountain road in silence. A day had passed since the fight in the cemetery. The paramedics hauled Larry out of the woods, leaving Paula and Angie to answer questions. On the record, the three of them went out into the woods for a late night hike, and Larry fell off a ledge, puncturing his stomach on a tree branch in the process. The girls helped him walk as far as they could before the blood loss left him unable to stand. It was a weak explanation, but no one had any reason to question them further. Larry was incredibly fortunate and the branch had not done significant damage to any internal organs, though he very nearly bled to death. Angie's makeshift tourniquet saved his life. A couple blood transfusions, several stitches, and a round of antibiotics to help fight infection had him stable and scheduled to be discharged the following day.

When things settled down and the doctor and nurses cleared out, Paula told Larry what happened in the cemetery. He listened gravely to her descriptions of her mother, father, and brother. She told him about the smell of honeysuckle and the cool energy radiating from the crucifix. He beamed with pride. She told him how the demon reacted to being hit with the crucifix, how Lonny freed her mother and father from their bindings, and how Angie cast the final blow.

"I'm so proud of you two," he said. "Somehow I knew Candy would be with us. It's like I said, faith is a powerful thing. *Family* is a powerful thing."

Now, with the afternoon sun drifting low in the sky, Paula steered her car onto the dirt road leading to Albert Crenshaw's shack. Before she could go back home, she needed him to know what happened.

The old cabin came into view and Paula parked the car. She climbed out, Angie following suit, and they approached the porch. The front door creaked open and Crenshaw stepped out into the fading light. He wore the same clothes he'd worn on their first visit, and his beard was even more disheveled, if that were even possible. He squinted at the girls for a moment, then recognition crossed his face.

"Didn't expect to see y'all again."

"We beat it," Paula said.

"Did ya, now? Not without a loss, I wonder? Where's your Daddy, girl?"

"He's okay. He's at the hospital, but he's gonna be fine."

"Ain't that somethin'." Crenshaw spat a wad of tobacco juice into the grass and scratched his beard. "How'd you do it?"

Paula told the story in its entirety. Crenshaw listened intently without interruption. When she finished, a moment of silence held between them. He looked around the woods, then back at the girls.

"And you ain't seen nothing or felt nothing since?"

"No," Paula replied. "It's gone."

"I ain't never been one to say I know everything. Just because I ain't never seen it done don't mean it can't be done."

"I wanted you to know. In case it ever comes back—or something like it."

"Not many folks come looking for help of that nature, but I thank ya all the same. I'm glad you found a way. Good to know the light still fights the dark from time to time."

Paula nodded. A weight had been lifted from her, and it finally felt like this was over. "Take care, Mr. Crenshaw," she said and walked back to the car. Angie hurried after her, obviously eager to leave.

Crenshaw watched them go, then called out before they opened the door. "You there, girl," he said, pointing a finger toward Angie, "it was you that gave the final blow?"

Angie nodded.

"The demon grabbed you, she said. Grabbed your ankle. Were ya hurt?"

"Just a scratch, really. Hurt for a day or so, but it's fine now."

"Healing up, okay?"

Angie looked down at her ankle and the faint red scar wrapping around it. "Yeah, no problem."

Crenshaw only nodded in reply. Paula got in the driver seat and closed the door. Angie stood on the passenger side staring curiously at Crenshaw.

"Why do you ask?" Angie called.

"No reason," Crenshaw said. "Y'all take care, now."

Angie stared at him for a moment longer, the setting sun casting bright rays of light on her face, flashing yellow on her eyes. Crenshaw held her gaze. A smile teased the corners of her mouth and she dropped into the car. He watched it pull away, tail lights disappearing into the trees.

"Oh, you wicked bitch," Crenshaw whispered, then walked back inside the cabin.

ACKNOWLEDGMENTS

Down Home is my second novella. Writing this one was a different experience than writing Chamberlain. I wasn't worried anymore whether or not I could write a story this long. The goal was to write a book that was as good or hopefully better than the last. I won't be so bold to say Down Home is better than The Doors of Chamberlain, but I like to think my skill as a writer has improved. You be the judge.

As always, many thanks go to my editor, Brandon Appelgate. He truly pushes my writing to the next level, makes me question every sentence, and doesn't hold back if something doesn't work. This is a better book because of him.

Matt Wildasin blew me away with the cover art. This was a first swing homerun, and I couldn't be happier with the results. I can't recommend him enough if you're looking for quality cover art.

Thank you to my beta readers Chuck Buda and Don Tackett. I always appreciate your feedback.

Writing a book takes a lot of time and support. I'm blessed to have a group of people to back me up. Always first, my wife, Jessie. Her support and pride in what I do is endlessly important. I could ramble on about all the people and how they support what I do. Whether it's texts and calls, or spreading the word, I appreciate all of you. Matt Wildasin, Chuck Buda, Brandon Applegate, Don Tackett, Simon Paul Wilson, Jason Meuschke, Raul Sanchez, Erica Robyn, Alex Bailey, Alex Norcross, JC Walsh, to name a few.

And, of course, thank you, reader. If you made it this far, I hope you enjoyed your trip Down Home, and I hope you'll come back for the next ride.

ABOUT THE AUTHOR

Steve L Clark is an author of horror and dark fiction from Southwest Ohio where he lives with his beautiful wife and three wonderful children. He is the author of The Doors of Chamberlain, The Collapse of Ordinary, and a contributing author to the anthology Dark Words: Stories of Urban Legends and Folklore edited by Matt Wildasin, all of which are available now on Amazon.

Follow Steve on Twitter @SteveLC8349 for updates on future projects.

www.ingramcontent.com/pod-product-compliance
Lightning Source LLC
Chambersburg PA
CBHW030006010826

48973CB00009B/2692